THE
COLOURS
OF
BIRDS

Anita,
Thank you for
being here
tonight!
all my best
wishes,
Rebecca
Ross

THE COLOURS OF BIRDS

Rebecca Higgins

TIGHTROPE BOOKS

Tightrope Books
#207-2 College Street,
Toronto Ontario, Canada M5G 1K3
tightropebooks.com
bookinfo@tightropebooks.com

EDITOR: Deanna Janovski
COVER DESIGN: David Jang
COVER PHOTO: David Clode
LAYOUT DESIGN: David Jang

Canada Council   Conseil des arts
for the Arts   du Canada

ONTARIO ARTS COUNCIL
CONSEIL DES ARTS DE L'ONTARIO
an Ontario government agency
un organisme du gouvernement de l'Ontario

Produced with the assistance of the Canada Council for the Arts and the Ontario Arts Council.

Library and Archives Canada Cataloguing in Publication

Higgins, Rebecca, 1977-, author
    The colours of birds / Rebecca Higgins.

Short stories.
ISBN 978-1-988040-43-1 (softcover)

    I. Title.

PS8615.I369C65 2018   C813'.6   C2018-902530-1

for my parents and their parents

CONTENTS

Stoplight

IT WAS NOT A GOOD OMEN WHEN WE KILLED A GUY ON THE WAY to the wedding. Not on purpose, of course. One minute, Lu was pouring champagne for me, and Carmen was leaning back taking a photo of us, and the next minute we slammed into something, hard. The driver started yelling—"Fuck! Fuck!"—and there was champagne all over my dress. Carmen's face was grey. One of Steve's sisters was saying, "What happened? What the hell happened?" and another one of them was trying to get out, but the door was stuck or locked or something. Lu's hand was bleeding.

"Oh God, this can't get on your dress!" she said, wrapping her hand in her bridesmaid dress. Now that's friendship, I thought later.

I felt really weird, like I was going to choke on my heartbeat. My hairline started itching really badly, and my lips felt thick. The driver radioed his dispatch. We heard him say, voice quivering, "I think I hit something." The radio crackled. He replaced the radio and got out of the car, telling us to stay inside.

We did, but he left the driver-side door open, so we could hear everything anyway, even if we couldn't see it.

"Oh, fuck. Oh. Oh no. Sir? Sir?" And then we heard him calling 911 on his cellphone, saying, "I think this guy's dead," and as it turned out, he was.

He'd run out fast into the road, against the light, and the driver couldn't stop in time, poor guy. Both of them, poor guys. There was something wrong with the dead one, like he was drunk or high or maybe there was something mixed up about his brain. We never did find out exactly what because the limo company dealt with whatever happened after.

Some of the girls got out to look while we waited for the police. I think Carmen was helping to direct traffic in the meantime. She's very responsible. Lu stayed with me, and I didn't argue when she said I shouldn't get out and look. I didn't want to see the guy anyway, because for the rest of my life, whenever I thought of my wedding day, I'd remember that: a sprawled person in dirty, torn clothes with limbs bent backwards and his face raw and ripped apart, lying on top of a dark stain in the middle of the street. Thing is, I do always think of that whenever I think of my wedding day, and I didn't even see it. It's actually been worse not seeing it. I should check with Carmen and see what he really looked like because I'm sure it's not as bad as the bloodbath I've got in my head.

A few of Steve's sisters came back to the car, and they were all crying.

"It's horrible. You should see for yourself," one of them said, the one that likes me the least.

Lu's bleeding hand was still in her dress, but her other hand was holding mine. "We're staying inside," she said firmly.

Steve's parents had rented one of those enormous Hummer limo things that we would usually make fun of, but because Steve has so many sisters and they all needed to be in the wedding party, we didn't have much of a choice. Our people wouldn't fit in a regular limo. If it were up to me, we would have just taken cabs there, or maybe borrowed a few cars, but Steve's mother had her fingerprints all over this thing from the beginning, probably even before Steve proposed.

On the way to the wedding, it was only the girls and the driver in the gigantic vehicle. We'd meet everybody else at the church, and after the ceremony part, the boys would get in and we'd all drive to the reception together. I had suggested we just all go together in the first place, but Steve's mother started freaking out about what bad luck it was for the bride and groom to go to the church together. I'm pretty sure killing someone on the way to your wedding is also bad luck, but Steve's mother wasn't there for me to ask.

Somebody called Steve, and probably his mother, to say we were going to be late because we couldn't leave before giving statements to the police. We probably all said versions of the same thing, so I don't know why they had to interview all of us girls individually. I felt for the driver, though. He was pacing around, smoking cigarette after cigarette, talking into his cellphone. I noticed when he hung up from one of the calls that his hands were shaking. He was having a worse day than I was.

They sent another limo to come and get us, this time a reasonably sized one because there were no other Hummer limos left. They'd have to take us in two trips to the reception. But this was not the greatest upset of the day. You'd think so, the way Steve's mother reacted when we finally made it to the church.

"This is awful. This limo is way too small, and everybody's going to be kept waiting afterwards. I just wanted everything to go smoothly today!" she said, fluttering her hands like she was about to take flight, which would have been nice.

"It's not the worst thing that could happen. Just ask the guy we left on the road back there," said Carmen. She's gutsy, but she was also not looking down the barrel of being this woman's daughter-in-law.

Steve's mother frowned and shook her head and said, "Well of course not, I feel for that poor man; what a terrible thing," but it was too little too late for sure.

I love Carmen. She's never afraid to say what she thinks. Sometimes I wish I'd married her.

You'd think that this would have made me stop and think about what I was about to do. I had plenty of time to change my mind in between the accident and standing at the front of the church beside Steve. I could have backed out any time between those two moments. But the momentum of the thing kept propelling me forward. Lu knew me better than anybody except Carmen, and when it was just us in the limo, her bloody hand in the poufy dress Steve's mother had chosen, she said quietly: "If you don't want to do this today, we don't have to. We can get out of it."

I looked at her, and her eyes were so soft and kind I knew that if I backed out she'd love me just the same as she did right now. But the momentum seemed an impossible obstacle. I couldn't see a way out. Everyone was expecting us. Late, now, but expecting us. Steve and his mother would be furious. My parents would probably be pissed too. I have always hated disappointing people. It's a problem. One time with an ex-boyfriend, I pretended I liked oatmeal for an entire year, choking it down every morning so I wouldn't hurt his feelings. So here was Lu—and a dead guy in the street—telling me it was okay to walk away, but I still couldn't do it. Though in retrospect, the huge whoosh of joy I felt when I considered it, just for a second, should have been a sign.

A few years after we killed the guy/got married, I walked into the kitchen, and Steve and his mother were sitting at the table. They stopped talking when I walked in, which wasn't unusual, so I ignored them and headed over to the fridge. The photos on the fridge were gone, and instead there was a clipping, neatly cut out of a magazine, taped near the handle. It was faded, and the paper was yellowing, but I could still see it clearly: a white plastic thing that looked like a small humidifier, with speech bubbles coming out of it: "No wonder you're getting fat!" "Stop eating, you pig!" The product description next to the photo read: "Talking refrigerator to keep your wife slim and you happy." Steve and his mother burst out laughing. "Wish we could still get those!" Steve said, or maybe it was his mother. I left the room but not before grabbing the chips on top of the fridge. No way was I going to give them the satisfaction.

By then something had shifted a bit in me. I still cared about disappointing people who were outside of our marriage, but I didn't give a shit about disappointing Steve and his mother. I sort of relished it. It was the one thing about us that came easy.

I didn't want kids and Steve did. To this day, I'm still not sure if I didn't want to have kids at all, or I didn't want kids with Steve. Either way, this caused a huge fight.

"You never thought to mention this before?" Steve said, his face blotching an ugly red.

I got out of bed to distance myself from that face.

"I thought we already talked about it," I lied. Of course we hadn't talked about it. It was the oatmeal all over again but this time with my uterus.

"This is what normal people do. Get married. Have kids." Steve was trying to keep his voice steady, I could tell, but his face was getting blotchier by the second.

I didn't say anything and stayed near the door, fiddling with stuff on the dresser—a pot of night cream, the lighter I used for candles and my secret cigarettes. Steve sighed.

"Think about it a little bit more, maybe, okay, honey? You don't want to regret it when you're older. Maybe you'll change your mind."

"Maybe," I said.

I didn't change my mind, but I got pregnant anyway.

I put my foot down when Steve wanted to name the baby after his mother.

"No way," I said, lips and teeth in a tight line.

Steve saw my face, and maybe he figured this was one he'd better let me win. He'd won the war, after all. Our baby was in his arms, there in the hospital. And I loved her when she was born and afterwards, of course I did. She was gorgeous, too, black hair and blue eyes, looking up at us all fresh and new and open, completely undisappointed.

"I'm naming her Carmen," I said, and Steve let me have that one.

In those early years, sometimes I'd take Little Carmen over to Big Carmen's house, and watching them together made my heart fall out. Carmen was so good with my daughter, crouching down and talking to her face to face, asking her about her favourite animal in a human tone of voice instead of that horrible baby-talk Steve's mother used with her. When the Carmens leaned their heads together over a book, I imagined a different life, where I'd be pulling open the door of a nonjudgemental fridge to make us dinner, and the girls would be laughing together in the other room, and the guy on the road wasn't dead, and Steve's mother was nowhere, and it was just the Carmens and me.

Sensitive

OLIVE IS FED UP WITH HER SENSITIVE PLANT. THE GUY IN
the store said give it lots of light. So Olive's got Mim (short for
mimosa pudica) in the sunniest part of the apartment and still the
plant seems unhappy. The guy in the store said all you need to
do is water it once a week (probably just trying to make the sale,
Olive thinks later, but unfortunately not at the time). She brought
Mim home on Friday, and by Monday the soil was already dry
and Mim was not looking well. Olive gave her a drink and hoped
for the best. Water seemed to perk Mim up temporarily, but a
day later she was drooping again, and now most of the leaves are
shrivelled up and dry, while some of them close to the soil look
yellow, like their little livers are jaundiced. Maybe Mim drank too
much too fast and is hungover.

　　In the week since she brought her home, Olive has given
the sensitive plant everything she was supposed to. There is
absolutely no reason for Mim to be this moody. Olive's pissed that
she's not more resilient. This is not the metaphor she hoped it
would be.

Maybe the stress of moving was too much for Mim. When Olive
found her in the store, she wasn't going home straight away, so the
guy put the plant in a white plastic bag and said it would be fine.
Olive took her new plant to the movies. The theatre was otherwise
empty, so the plant got a seat to herself. Olive pulled the plastic
down so Mim could breathe better. She put her purse beside her so

the seat wouldn't snap shut and crush Mim.

The movie was very stressful to watch, about a coup in an unnamed country in Latin America where suddenly everybody is trying to kill all white Americans for reasons not properly explained. It was quite racist, and Olive was embarrassed that she chose this for Mim's first movie. Being from Latin America originally herself, Mim would hate this simplistic, xenophobic portrayal of her home. But Olive had already paid, so they kept watching.

Olive looked over at Mim a few times. Her leaves were still closed, as they had been since she'd chosen the plant, but it was night, so maybe she was sleeping rather than closing her eyes against the violence, as Olive was doing enough to make her consider walking out. But it might upset Mim more to move her again so quickly. At one point, Olive left Mim to go to the bathroom during a particularly terrifying scene where the main guy was throwing his children from one roof to another. When she got back, the children were safe and Mim hadn't moved.

Olive doesn't watch the news because it makes her feel very stressed out. Sometimes at work somebody will say something about a storm or corporate takeover or stock plunge or plane crash. Olive just shakes her head and mirrors whatever the other person's face is doing. If it's a disaster of some kind (which it almost always is, which is why Olive doesn't watch the news), she murmurs something like "It's so awful" and extracts herself quickly. It is popular practice to be informed. Olive chooses not to be, but she doesn't want to get into a conversation about how important it is to know what's going on in the world. One of those conversations can be almost as stressful as watching the news in the first place.

The chestnut tree in front of the building has leaf blotch. It's a disease it gets every year about this time, and it is very upsetting. It doesn't kill the tree or permanently damage it, but every August the leaves start browning. It's depressing, like slicing open an avocado and finding it rotten inside. Brown when you're expecting green. If you just stared at that tree all day you'd think it was the end of October or something, and Olive hates anything that hastens the winter.

Maybe Mim's mood is low because of the leaf blotch. At this time of year, Olive usually keeps the blinds shut more often than not so she doesn't have to look at the ugly tree. But Mim needs the sunlight, so Olive keeps the blinds open and tries not to spend too much time looking out the window.

When she checks on her on Saturday morning, Mim doesn't seem too bad, considering. What's left of her is green and open, leaning towards the light. Olive's irritation withers and drops. She wells up a little. Mim is tougher than she looks.

Dead leaves are lying on the saucer and some have dropped onto the ground. Olive collects them and clears them away. Mim does not need to be standing in her own death.

Harriet calls.

"Can we come by today? I need adult company."

"Okay," Olive says and tells herself it will be.

"Around noon?"

Olive starts to panic and pace. What will she feed them? What does Jake eat or not eat? It must be her turn to say something. She gathers up some words and is trying to put them in an order that will make sense to Harriet, when her sister sighs and says: "It's fine. We'll eat first and come at two. That okay?"

"Okay," Olive says quickly and hangs up before things change.

Olive finds children unsettling. She loves Jake, sort of, because he's her nephew, but he's exhausting to be around. How Harriet manages it is a mystery, but Harriet has always been more even-keel than Olive. When they were kids, their dad took them through a car wash. In the car of course, but Olive was absolutely terrified, sticking her tiny fingers up to the seam where the glass met the frame to make sure no water was coming in. Harriet was reading a comic book during the ordeal. By the time they got through the car wash, Olive's face was as wet as the car and her chest felt like it was full of stones. Harriet looked over at her and sighed, then tapped their dad on the shoulder.

"Olive's upset, Dad," she said, and the next time they went through the car wash, Olive got out and stood by the hose that fills tires with air. Harriet stayed in the car and read a comic book.

Harriet doesn't read comic books anymore, and she sighs more than she used to. She's not so skinny these days, and there's grey in her hair, but otherwise she hasn't changed much. She's the calm one. Olive finds this very annoying sometimes, but she generally doesn't say so. Jake, on the other hand, is not that calm. He runs a lot and seems to fall over without bumping into anything, and he makes a lot of noise. He seems to enjoy banging things. Olive looks around the room and wonders what he's going to do with himself when they visit. She digs out a deck of cards and some gum and hopes that will be enough.

When they arrive, Harriet hugs her with one arm, Jake in the other.

"I've got some gum and cards for Jake," Olive says.

Harriet looks at her strangely. "Jake's two, Olive. He can't have gum."

"Oh, of course, I forgot," Olive lies. Two year olds can't have gum?

Harriet and Jake follow her into the living room, and everybody sits down. Jake only stays sitting for half a second, though, before he slips off the couch and starts kicking the legs of it and then stomping on the floor. He's laughing. It seems fun for him. It is not fun for Olive. Her body scrunches up against the noise. Harriet sighs.

"Jakey, don't do that, okay, honey? I've brought some stuff for you to play with." She digs blocks and books and some soft animals out of a bag and gets Jake set up on the floor. Olive puts the gum and cards on the coffee table.

"Do you have any coffee?"

Of course. But please don't spill it or let Jake spill it. "Sure, I'll get it started."

When she gets back from putting the coffee on, the machine

clearing its throat and getting down to brewing, Jake is playing with the stuff that Harriet's pulled out for him with one hand, the other digging around in his nose. Harriet is staring out the window at the leaf blotch.

"That tree doesn't look that great."

"No."

"Have you talked to the landlord? Maybe the city can cut it down."

Olive bristles. "It doesn't look great, but it's healthy. It will be green again after the winter."

"But it's kind of ugly to look at."

Jake is wiping what comes out of his nose on the floor.

"It's fine. What's been going on with you?"

"Well, lots, but for one thing, Andrew's mother isn't doing so well."

Harriet's husband is a very good son to his mother, visiting her every day after work, but sometimes it makes it hard for Harriet, alone with Jake all the time. Olive feels for her sister, but being alone is not the part Harriet talks about.

"That's too bad."

"Yeah, sometimes when he goes in now, she thinks he's her other son, the one who died when he was little."

"I didn't know Andrew had a brother who died." This information makes Harriet's husband more interesting.

"Yeah, I don't know much about that; he never talks about it."

Shocking.

"Cwackers."

Harriet tries to ignore him.

"So you were saying that she thinks Andrew is his brother?" Olive has developed a skill she never needed before Jake's arrival. She is now a prompter.

"Yes, and—"

"CWAACCCKKEERRSS."

Behind him, near the window, Mim's leaves are closed even though it's the middle of the day. Olive doesn't blame her.

"Do you have any crackers? I brought grapes, but we ran out of the goldfish he likes."

"I might, but I don't think I have the goldfish."

"Whatever you have."

In the kitchen, Olive digs some stale saltines out of the back of the cupboard and puts them in some plastic Tupperware for the kid, who is starting to wail.

"Auntie Olive is getting you some crackers, okay?" Harriet says in a soothing voice to him, slightly muffled. She must have picked him up, her face in his hair. The wail shrinks to a whimper.

The coffee maker has stopped gurgling, and it smells deep and dark and comforting. Olive stands in front of the machine and breathes in, feeling her body loosen some.

"Hey, is this the new issue?" Harriet calls. She must be talking about the magazine on the coffee table. Olive loves when a magazine is just new, and she is looking forward to reading it later this afternoon, curled in a corner of the couch with tea that smells like vanilla and cinnamon.

"Yeah," Olive calls back. Normally she doesn't like anyone to read a new magazine before she gets to it—she likes the pages to be smooth and unfolded, the shiny pictures unseen by other eyes—but Harriet knows this, and Olive doesn't want to hear that sigh again.

"Go ahead," she says, knowing that Harriet is already flipping through it, reading the unread stories. She pours the cups of coffee—black for both of them—and puts them on a tray that Harriet gave her for a birthday a few years ago. She adds the Tupperware crackers. Jake is quiet now. Olive breathes in deeply, pauses, and breathes out, long and slow. Then she takes the tray into the living room.

Harriet is on the couch looking at the magazine, and Jake is over in the corner near Mim. Very close to Mim. Olive's stomach bottoms out. Still carrying the tray, she gets closer. Jake pulls a leaf and several more fall. He rips another leaf off and drops it onto Mim's plate, filling with leaf parts and bits of twig and dirt. Mim is nearly naked. Olive shivers and freezes. She wants to stop him but can't speak, just stands behind him with the tray, tears coming. Quiet things are suddenly loud, and Olive can hear Mim's parts as they hit the plate, as clearly as she can hear Harriet turning pages behind her.

My Dad and Me, and Everybody Else

EVERY DAY OF THE WEEK I STEAL BOOKS, BUT SUNDAYS ARE different. On Sunday nights, when other people are at AA meetings or watching nature programs or washing quilts at the laundromat, I take the books to a pond in the big park near my apartment. It's the swampy part of the pond, full of bulrushes and sludge. On Sunday nights, this part of the park is quiet and empty. I carry the books in a large red backpack, the kind other people use for camping. Before I leave the apartment, I take inventory of the backpack: books, duct tape, plastic bags. If it's been a particularly good week, I may fill and carry a few extra plastic bags full of books, too, doubled so they don't break on the way.

Sometimes I wonder if anyone's looking out their windows when I walk by with my red backpack every Sunday night. Maybe there's an old lady who spends a lot of time watching the neighbourhood through her bifocals, and maybe she thinks, "Oh, that nice boy must be coming back from another weekend at home. His mother must be so proud."

When I get to the pond, I check around, just to make sure, but I'm always alone. Then I drop the backpack on the grass and unload everything. Bibles and children's stories and thin volumes of poetry. I bundle the books into stacks and wrap them in the duct tape. I drop each stack into its own plastic bag. To each bag, I add rocks. I knot and double knot each bag, and add a final layer of tape to seal everything in. Then I fling the packages one by one into the pond like lead Frisbees. Sometimes they're especially heavy, and I have to use both arms to throw them in. I slip the bag onto my back while I check to make sure no books are floating up to the top of the pond.

Soon I'm going to have to find another dump site. Under the surface, the pile of books must be growing. At this rate, someday I'm going to toss in a package, and it'll just sit on the top of the underwater book mountain, not hidden at all.

On Mondays, Wednesdays, and Fridays, right after my shift finishes at three, I go to the library around the corner. I mill around, flip through magazines, pretend to use the computer catalogue. Sometimes I find a comfortable chair and take a nap. I check the schedule to see who's using the community rooms and when they'll be finished. The community rooms are in the basement. Seniors knit there, or children do their homework, leaned over by a volunteer. When a group finishes, I watch them from an upstairs window. I watch them stream out the front door and down the steps, some racing off alone, others strolling and chatting with friends from the group. Then I slip downstairs, as quickly as I can without being too obvious, and dip into the smaller of the rooms before the librarian comes down to lock the door. I pull the books out of my bag and from under my shirt. I slide open the window and push the books out onto the grass. Then I go upstairs and out of the building, grab the books off the ground, and head home.

I wander side streets on Saturdays, looking for yard sales (easy, but limited because they're seasonal). I browse the small sales but only work the big ones. For one thing, the big yard sales are more likely to have books. For another thing, the owners of the yard are more likely to be distracted, stuck haggling over the price of a ceramic elephant or a macramé plant holder. Too preoccupied to see me.

Sometimes I'll luck out and there will be a fire truck racing by or a stroller of twins, so the yard owner (and everybody else at the sale) is suddenly distracted. I'll lean over, pretending to flip through a crate of old records, and as I lean forward, I'll slip a few books into the bag I've got with me. Sometimes I'll even buy a record for good measure, even though I don't have a turntable.

Tuesdays and Thursdays are reserved for bookstore work. I was at a party once, caught in a conversation with somebody who worked at one of the big-box bookstores. He told me their theft detectors are just for show. That they don't even work. This information has proven very useful. I mostly stick to one location, the one nearest the park, because I don't want to push my luck with one of the bigger stores downtown. Sometimes I take the bus out to the suburbs and shop there. The trick is to walk out at medium speed. Too fast and you attract attention; too slow and people wonder. I usually check my phone or my watch, or look out intently at something on the street. This keeps my eyes occupied and my pace even as I leave, spines of books pressing into the flesh under my arms.

When I was growing up, our house was silent and filled with books. The living room was lined with floor-to-ceiling shelves. Nothing was organized, just crammed in there, regardless of subject or colour. In front of the bookshelves were more mounds. Books lined the hall to the kitchen, and under the kitchen table there were teetering piles that used to fall over when I kicked my legs at breakfast. The staircase between the main and second floors started off clear, but when I was a teenager, the books started going up the stairs too. At first they were only on one side, under the bannister, so it was easy enough to get upstairs or down without knocking over the piles. Later, in the year or two before I left, there was only a narrow pathway up the stairs, flanked on either side by heaps of books.

The only sound was the *ffftt* of pages turning. It was just my dad and me. He worked at a library all day and then came home to another one. I don't remember how my father was before my mother left. She left when I was three. I heard the story once, from my aunt right before she died, the pain pushing out all of her unsaid things, I guess. Anyway, this is what my aunt said:

"Your mother came home that night. It was late, maybe close to midnight. She was a secretary, and her work finished at five thirty, but she'd gone out with the insurance people after the office closed. She walked over to where your father was. He was in the living room, reading in his recliner. She took off all of her clothes, right in front of the chair, and stood in front of him. He kept reading and didn't look up. She stood there naked, quiet, looking at him. He didn't look up. She waited for twenty minutes, just standing there. Then she picked up her clothes, dressed, and went upstairs. Your father didn't move. You were asleep. She kissed you on your head, packed enough things to manage, and left."

Listening to that story made me uncomfortable. I guess it's good I don't remember her because when I think of that story the woman's face is a smudge without features, like she might not be related to me at all.

After my aunt told me that, she said to send my father in. He was in the waiting room, reading. He finished the page before he stood up, closed the book on his finger, and went to see his dying sister. His reading glasses were still on his face as he turned to shut the door of her room.

I didn't do all that well in high school, but not too bad considering I did everything I could to avoid reading. I took a lot of classes that didn't require much of it: all the maths, music, art, gym. English was the hardest to fake my way through, but I rented most of the required readings and watched my way through the syllabus. *Lord of the Flies*, *Hamlet*, *To Kill a Mockingbird*—all of that stuff was easy to find on video.

I passed everything and graduated with the other kids. Passing was good enough. It's not like I wanted to go to university, but I had to figure something out. I needed a job, that was for sure. I wasn't picky. All I wanted was a peaceful, bookless life.

When I got the job at the shredding company the summer after graduation, I was happy. There was "room to grow" at the company, my manager told me after they offered me a position as a customer-service rep. Meaning I could stay there and eventually make more money, maybe even be a manager someday. Best of all it meant I could move out. Soon.

I saved up every cent and moved out six months after I started working. I didn't take much, just my clothes and stuff, and moved into a basement apartment, already furnished. I didn't stand in front of my dad when I left. I didn't even look at him, really. I said goodbye and waved over my shoulder and left him to his library. He probably didn't look up, but I can't say I turned around to check.

It's not like we never spoke again. We'll have an awkward phone call every few months, basically the same conversation every time.

"Hi, Mark. It's Dad."

"Yep."

"How are you?"

"Good. How are you?"

"Oh, you know. Busy."

I never understand this. My dad's retired now, and he doesn't have any friends or anybody to go out with, and the only activity he likes to do is read. How busy can the guy be? But maybe it's just one of the things we say to each other. My dad and me, and everybody else.

"How's the job? Still liking it?" he asks.

"Yeah, it's good. Nice people." And I love being in the document destruction business, I think. It's true, but he won't get that, or he will and it will hurt him, so I try not to say that very often.

We might say a few more things, about the weather or something, and then one of us makes an excuse to get off the phone, and the other one agrees, and we say goodbye.

Every year for my birthday, my dad sends me a book in the mail. I can't help reading the titles before I get rid of them. Two years ago, he sent me a novel by some Russian guy I'd never heard of. I took that book to work and shredded it on my break. It went quick. It got rid of it, but I don't do it that way anymore. The pond is a better high.

I started doing it around my birthday last year. My dad sent me a dictionary of symbolism. I didn't get it. What did that have to do with anything? It would be a bad present even if I were a reader. That book arrived on a Friday, and I wouldn't be at work again until Monday, and the last thing I wanted was that book in the apartment over the weekend. So I started walking around looking for a good place to dump it. I could have just left it on a lawn or in the garbage, but they have those trash cans now with the round holes, no good for squishing books into. And if I left it on a lawn, it might have still been there the next time I walked by, and I just wanted to get rid of the thing. So I kept on walking, holding on to that book, wanting to get it as far away from my apartment as I could. I wandered into the park, and there were wider garbage cans there, but I had the idea by then, and I kept walking with that book until I got to the pond.

Getting it to sink took a while. First time, I drew back my arm and flung that stupid dictionary with all the strength I had, but it didn't get very far out at all, and then it just fucking floated there. I got right to the edge and leaned way out and pulled it back in, dripping and heavier than ever, and figured I'd better weight it down somehow. I left it under a bush and went to get a few supplies from a convenience store across from the park, feeling like a serial killer, determined and guiltless. Excited.

When I got back, I shoved the wet book in a bag with a few stones and wrapped the whole thing up with tape. And then I whipped that thing away from me. It flew out of my hands, way out into the water. It splashed and went down, and I felt my shoulders relax and something releasing in my chest. It felt better than shredding. I felt like I did when I went out with a couple of guys one Friday after work, and one of them gave me a few Xanax at the bar, and I gulped them down with my beer and, after a bit, I felt good. This felt like that except I wasn't sleepy at all. I was relaxed and awake at the same time, and I couldn't remember feeling like that before.

It's Tuesday, and I'm on my way across the parking lot to check the truck before my first customer call. I hear my name and turn around. Susan from human resources is having a cigarette near the front door. I wave and she comes over. Susan's okay, not too chatty like some of the other people at work, and her tits usually look great in whatever top she's wearing. Today she's wearing something shiny and black, and the light glints off it as she walks over.

"It's your birthday this week, right?" she says, blowing smoke out of the side of her mouth and up.

"How'd you know that?"

She tilts her head. "I'm in human resources, Mark. I have access to ALL of the personnel files." She does a fake witch's cackle and throws her head back, and the skin of her throat looks smooth and like it might taste good.

"Do you want to go out on Friday for it? We can get a bunch of people together." She looks down, dropping her cigarette on the cement and grinding it out with the toe of her black, shiny shoe. Maybe that guy with the Xanax will come again, and maybe Susan will get a little bit drunk, and it might be a good birthday this year.

"Sure, Susan. Good idea."

"Great! I'll get something organized." She smiles and turns and heads back to the office. I watch her hips and her ass until she gets to the building, and then I get to work.

On Thursday evening, I come home from shopping and head straight to the back of the building to put all the books in the garage as usual. The other two tenants in our little building never seem to use the garage, but I keep the books covered with a tarp just in case. All that pile of books would get me is a lot of questions.

After I'm finished out back, I walk around to the front door. There's a manila envelope sticking out of my mailbox. I don't even need to look at the return address—there is only one person who would send me a package this size and shape.

I should take it out back and stuff it under the tarp with the others, but I'm curious to see how off the mark my dad will be this year. Maybe it'll be a good story to tell Susan at the bar.

I don't want the neighbours watching me open the envelope and wondering what I'm up to. So I take the envelope inside and downstairs, where the light is better, figuring I'll open it here in the hallway, see what the old man came up with this year, and slip out the back door to put the thing under the tarp in the garage until Sunday.

I rip open the envelope, and the sound of paper coming apart reminds me of work. I pull out the book. On the green cover, a little boy is looking up at a falling apple, holding out his arms to catch it.

In the memory, my mother isn't there, and it doesn't feel like she's just in the kitchen or the backyard, so it must have happened after she left. I'm sitting next to my dad on the couch, and we're reading the book together. We've read it before, because on some pages, he's quiet and lets me fill in the words, even though I can't read yet.

My dad says that the boy loved the tree.

"... very much." I say.

The tree loves the boy even when he gets older. He uses her apples to make money, her branches to build a house, and her trunk to make a boat and sail away.

My dad reads that the tree was happy.

"... but not really." I say.

My dad pulls me a little closer. We keep reading. At the end of the story, the tree is only an old stump, and the boy is an old man. The only thing he wants is to sit and rest, and he sits on what's left of the tree, and the tree is happy.

When we are finished the story, I want my dad to read it again. I flip through the book backwards to get to the beginning, and the tree turns from a stump to a trunk to a tree, getting bigger as the boy gets smaller.

My dad begins the story again, and I am happy.

There must be something wrong with him, some kind of terminal thing. Why would he send such bullshit books every other year, and this year send one that actually has something to do with me? Suddenly, I'm furious. What an asshole. Is he trying to get me to visit more? Why doesn't he get his head out of the fucking books for a second and be straight with me?

For the first time, I wonder if I'm not the only person he's sending books to. What if he actually knows where my mother is and sends her books, too, every year? What if he sends her novels about dismembered marriages or how-to books about surviving as a single parent? Maybe he goes to visit my aunt's grave and puts books at her gravestone instead of flowers. I'm pissed, but also something feels weird in my stomach, and I have to get that book out of here, off this property, away from me, and it can't wait till Sunday.

My hands are getting itchy. I've still got a balled-up plastic bag in my pocket from shopping, and I put the book in there. The bag is some thin, crummy plastic, and the green cover is glowing through it. I can still read the title even though I don't want to, but at least it's not touching me anymore. I stick the bagged book under my arm, pull the front door of the building shut behind me, and start walking towards the pond.

On the way there, I try to think about shredding or yard sales or Susan or Xanax or anything that isn't the memory, but it keeps sliding back in and pushing all the nicer thoughts out of the way. I can hear the *ffftt* of the pages and my dad's voice and my own in the spaces between.

There's nobody near the pond, at least nobody who lets themselves be seen. It's quiet enough to hear the rustle of plastic as I move. The light is changing fast. I forgot to bring tape, and I can't find a decent-sized rock, so I just stuff some pebbles into the bag with the book and knot it. I throw it as hard as I can away from me, aiming for the middle of the pond, but it splashes into the water only a few metres from shore. Not close enough to grab but not far enough away from me, either. I stand on the shore and consider hunting around for a long branch or even wading out there to bring it back and try again, but while I'm standing there thinking about it, I see something bob up and float. The green glows through the thin plastic, brighter than swamp sludge.

I feel the tears coming up my throat like vomit or words when I'm drunk, and then the pond is blurry, but I can still see the book, and I'm starting to panic, and I wish I had a Xanax, but instead I just sit down on the closest thing I can find to a bench, and it's a stump, and then I cry harder.

Charlene at Lunchtime

WHEN PEOPLE START TALKING ABOUT WHAT COMES OUT OF PETS and kids, Charlene takes her lunch to the bathroom and eats it in a stall.

Today, Charlene walks into the lunchroom, and Roberta is telling everyone about her kid's first poop in the toilet. "We've been working on this forever, so this is so exciting for us! Soon she won't even need a diaper anymore!"

Roberta's face is red like she's working on her own first-time dump. Charlene starts counting to twenty slowly in her head.

Angela from human resources nods. So does Tina. Even Jerry nods in Roberta's direction as she talks, although he's looking more at the door than at her. He's eating something steaming. Tina says, "I wish Bailey learned as quickly as your little one! He might not be ready to sleep outside the crate after all."

Twenty.

"Oh, shit, I forgot to get back to Mr. Endleson!" Charlene says and backs out of the lunchroom. Nobody glances at her except Jerry, whose expression reminds her of a POW she saw interviewed once on TV.

In her cubicle, she arranges her pens across the desk, end to end, before scooping them up and dropping them into a plastic vase the last person left behind. For good measure, she writes "call Mr. Endleson" on a Post-it note on her desk, in case anybody asks about it later. Then she heads to the bathroom, cucumber sandwich in her purse.

She's just sat down in a stall and is pulling the tinfoil away from her sandwich when somebody comes in. Charlene freezes. The hiss of pee, then a flush. Water splashes into the sink. Charlene waits for the door to bang shut; the bathroom is so quiet she can hear her own breath.

Charlene's stomach gurgles. She checks her watch, and it's nearly one. She opens her legs and pours a gulpful of Diet Pepsi between her knees and into the toilet. The woman sniffs and goes out. Charlene digs into her cucumber sandwich. She drinks what's left of the Diet Pepsi. When she's swallowed the last bit of sandwich, she shakes the crumbs into the toilet and smooths the tinfoil flat against her thigh. She tugs too hard and rips it, and there's no sense in saving it now, so she crumples it up until it's a tiny ball with sharp edges. She flips open the lid of the napkin disposal and pushes in the tinfoil and her Diet Pepsi can, in case anyone else comes in just as she's leaving the stall with an armful of lunch things. But no one does come in, and the clatter of the can against the bin is louder than Charlene would like.

It's the middle of the afternoon, and Charlene is lining up her pens in a row. She finds this very relaxing. Back to back like when they're fresh, when the package has just been opened, and they all have their caps on, and everything is neat.

"Hey, Charlene. Christmas exchange?"

Startled, Charlene knocks some of the pens to the ground. She bends over to pick them up and bonks her head on the desk as she's straightening back up.

"Ooh, are you okay? I hate doing that."

Maria Jose is standing beside the desk with a bowl in her hand. She's looking at Charlene with her eyebrows scrunched up in concern. Charlene's stomach feels like those somersaulting greyhounds her cousin put on YouTube.

"I'm okay."

Another pen rolls off the edge of the desk, and Maria Jose squats to pluck it off the carpet. Her hair is black and straight with smudges of white at her temples and along the part in the middle of her head. Every few months, Maria Jose comes to work with the grey gone again, her hair shimmery and sleek, but it never seems to last; within a few weeks her roots are showing, and the white threads are back. If Charlene manages to get a seat close to her in the lunchroom, she tries to count the grey hairs on Maria's head, but it's very difficult to do unless she's sitting right beside her and Maria Jose is absorbed in conversation with somebody else.

Maria Jose listens to people like they're interesting. In the lunchroom, she leans forward and puts her chin on her fist when someone is telling a story. When she laughs, she opens her mouth wide, and if Charlene is sitting across from her, she can see inside: neat Tic Tac teeth and black fillings on her molars. Her pink tongue.

Maria Jose never talks about what comes out of pets or kids.

She puts the pen back on the desk.

"This is for the Christmas exchange," says Maria Jose, jiggling the bowl so Charlene can see the bits of paper inside, softly rustling.

"Oh, should I put my name in there?" Charlene asks, pointing at the bowl with her chin.

"I already did. It's no problem." Maria Jose smiles. "Go ahead and take one."

Charlene swims her fingers around in the bowl and pulls out a slip of paper.

Tina.

"Oops, I got my own name. Can I do it again?"

Jerry.

Charlene considers picking again, but twice in a row will seem suspicious, so she folds the paper into a tiny square and puts it in her pocket.

Maria Jose tucks the bowl under her arm and fixes Charlene's pens so they're all lined up properly again. As she leans over the desk, her earrings dangle and clink like wind chimes.

They are made of tiny copper leaves and silver feathers and wire. The greyhounds flop over again.

The next day, Charlene spends most of the day looking up gingerbread houses on the internet. She skips the lunchroom/bathroom altogether and eats her sandwich in front of the computer.

The computer world is full of elegant, complicated gingerbread houses. One is a replica of the White House in happier times, with little Obamas in chocolate icing. On another site, she finds an office skyscraper, tall and beige and precarious. She remembers how stressful it was playing Jenga as a kid, pulling each block out as slowly as she could, feeling startled and disappointed when the tower inevitably collapsed.

Baking is not Charlene's forte. Not her skill set, in office talk. Still, she is drawn to the precision of it. She likes how unforgiving it is; if you don't measure things properly, the cake is ruined. She appreciates it when order is rewarded.

It is late in the afternoon when Charlene finds the house she will make for Maria Jose: a pretzel cabin. The perfect gingerbread house for country mice, the photo caption says. One Monday at lunchtime, Maria Jose said to Jerry, "Did you go to your cottage this weekend, Jerry?"

"I did, but it looks like I'm going to have to sell it," Jerry said, looking kind of sick and squinty.

"Oh, I'm so sorry," Maria Jose said, leaning forward and touching Jerry on the arm. "I know you love it up there."

"I do, but it's too expensive now, with Michael's tuition and all that," Jerry said into his Tupperware.

"I had a cabin once, but I had to give it up, too," Maria Jose said quietly. Jerry nodded, not looking up.

Making a gingerbread house can be broken down into several steps, Charlene reads. She copies the list from the internet, each step on its own index card, and then she straightens the pile and tucks it into her purse.

That night, after reviewing her index cards, Charlene lies in bed and thinks about gingerbread houses. There are a lot of problems to sort out or, at least, choices to make. For example, how is she going to add the water feature? There has to be a water feature. Once, Charlene overheard Maria Jose in the lunchroom saying to Tina, "I just feel so relaxed next to water, you know? It can be a swimming pool, even a little stream. It just calms me."

Maria Jose pulled her hair back, white strands shining. Charlene breathed in deeply and imagined she was catching a bit of Maria Jose's smell, a mix of fruit shampoo, onions, and wind.

Precisely one week before the Christmas exchange, Charlene starts building the gingerbread house. According to the first index card, she needs to build the base first using some cardboard covered in foil. She has this stuff at home already, so that's easy, but the internet says it's also important to cut out a template and tape it together before starting in with the gingerbread. Any kind of stiff paper will do. Charlene goes into the supply room at lunch and stuffs ten sheets of cardstock into her bag. On the subway home, she holds the bag flat against her so none of the pages get crumpled by other commuters.

At home in her little apartment, she sits down at her kitchen table-desk and tapes the first index card to its surface. She covers the lid of a banker's box with tinfoil, and the base is ready. Then, very carefully, she measures, traces, and cuts out two cardstock rectangles for the side walls then two smaller rectangles for the end walls. The gables and roof rectangles take a bit longer, but in an hour she has eight perfect cut-outs, ready for the next index card.

Charlene decides to take her time with the gingerbread house to make sure that it is perfect. She paces herself and goes to bed early.

The bulk food store is more cluttered than Charlene would like, and the aisles are too narrow. A small boy runs toward her, his mouth smudged with chocolate, and she has to turn sideways to avoid colliding with him. He careens around the corner, knocking a packet of rice crackers to the ground. Charlene waits until he is out of sight before she picks up the package and puts it back where it belongs.

Charlene is carrying a red plastic basket that bangs against her calf as she goes down the aisles. First she fills it up with white things: flour and royal icing mix to use as glue. Making the icing from scratch seems an unnecessary risk. Too much can go wrong, and the internet has assured her that the mix works just as well. Then she gathers all the brown ingredients, dumping scoops of pretzels into a filmy plastic bag and twisting a tie around its neck. Ground cinnamon, ginger, and cloves and dark molasses in a brown and yellow carton. She chooses some toffee bits and chocolate chips in case she needs them.

There aren't as many green things to collect, but it is a trickier task. Charlene needs an assortment of green candies, and the bins aren't organized by colour. So she has to lean over each bin of multicoloured candies and pick out the green ones with tongs. She sifts through the M&M's, gum drops, jelly beans, and Skittles. Finally, she scoops out all the blue Jolly Ranchers she can find.

At the cash, Charlene is nervous that she'll get in trouble for cherry-picking the candies, but the retirement-age lady standing at the register just says, "I like the green ones too, but more when they're lime. That green-apple flavour has nothing to do with nature."

"What flavour do you think the blue is supposed to be?" says a guy in the line behind Charlene.

The lady considers it. "It's not blueberry, is it? My grandkids just always say 'the blue flavour.'"

"My kid loves it, and she says it tastes like the sky," says the guy.

"That's adorable! How old is she?"

They are still talking as Charlene puts the receipt into her wallet and goes outside with her purchases. The sky is a strange shimmery grey. Charlene hurries down into the subway before it starts to rain.

The dry ingredients are easy enough to mix together, but creaming the butter and brown sugar until fluffy is more difficult. It's fluffy enough, in the end, but it's more like paste than clouds.

Ginger, cinnamon, cloves, pepper, salt, molasses.

Charlene mixes the dry and wet ingredients together like the index card tells her to. Her wrist is starting to ache from all of the stirring, the earned kind of ache, like after exercise.

Dividing the dough into thirds, Charlene wraps each chunk in name-brand plastic wrap she bought especially for the gingerbread house project. The index card tells her that she needs to put the dough in the fridge for at least one hour but that overnight is better. Charlene still has a few days to do the building, gluing, and decorating. There is plenty of time to finish the pretzel cabin for Maria Jose, with sky-flavoured water behind it.

In the lunchroom, Tina asks Roberta what she's doing for the holidays.

"Oh, you know, we do all of that Santa stuff. Our daughter just goes bananas for the stockings and that. What about you?"

"Well, we actually do a stocking for Bailey," Tina says around a mouthful of tuna sandwich.

"You do? That's so funny! What do you put in it?" Roberta asks, and Charlene stops listening.

Across the table, Maria Jose is saying something quietly to Jerry, who's nodding as he picks at his pasta. Then he looks straight at Maria Jose the way Charlene never has the nerve to do and says, "Thanks, Maria Jose. That means a lot." Maria Jose smiles at him, and the lines around her eyes are like how wind looks when it's drawn in children's books, still and moving at the same time.

The preheating oven is warming up the apartment enough for Charlene to be working in a t-shirt and shorts. After rolling out the dough, Charlene flours her palms, like a gymnast. She uses the paper template to help her make each piece of gingerbread exactly the right size and shape for the cabin, slides the baking sheets into the oven, and in fifteen minutes the gingerbread is done. Her apartment smells like Christmas movies and natural dandruff shampoo. Charlene lifts her arm and wipes her forehead to stop the sweat from dripping onto the gingerbread.

She mixes up the royal icing according to the instructions on the package and spoons the white globs into a pastry bag. She pipes the shape of the cabin onto the tinfoil base and then stands the first piece of gingerbread up, making sure it is well glued down before she adds the other three, one at a time, squeezing neat lines of icing up and down the hinges of the walls. The internet says it's easier to do this with an assistant. Charlene thinks of a sign she saw once in the front window of a dance studio: *Learn, with or without a partner*. She uses cans of beans and peas to support the pieces while she glues them all together with icing. One of the side walls leans like it might cave in, but Charlene straightens it and fortifies the base with the sweet glue.

She ties a blue ribbon around the roofless cabin and waits for it to dry.

"Are you going away for the holiday?" Maria Jose asks, leaning toward Charlene and dipping her sleeve in her bowl of soup. If it were Tina, she would at least sigh, and Roberta might get mad and even stomp out of the lunchroom, but Maria Jose just laughs. Charlene leans over the table to pass her a napkin.

"Thank you so much. I'm so clumsy," she says, blotting at the stain. Actually Maria Jose is the most graceful person in the office. She glides between the cubicles, skirt softly swishing, and, on her, dunking a sleeve in a bowl of soup is like a curtsy.

"I'm not doing much," Charlene says. "What about you?"

"My aunts and cousins are coming from home. Christmas is really important in El Salvador, and I don't think I'll be able to give them what they're used to." Maria Jose frowns a little and goes back to spooning the soup into her mouth.

Charlene pictures herself knocking on Maria Jose's door on Christmas Eve with a wagon of Salvadorean food in casserole dishes, multiple courses and meals perfectly prepared. "Everything's ready, just heat and serve," Charlene says graciously. Maria Jose wells up and reaches out to hug her. "This is so perfect. Please come in. Stay with us." Charlene nods, and Maria Jose brings the wagon into the house, the silver in her hair glinting in the light from the foyer.

Since she pulled Jerry's name out of Maria Jose's bowl of paper, Charlene has been mulling over how to handle the Jerry element of the Christmas exchange. She likes Jerry, mostly because of the shell-shocked expression he usually wears at lunchtime. She doesn't want him to be without a present, but the pretzel cabin can only be for Maria Jose. There is, of course, the uncomfortable thought that Maria Jose is going to get two presents: the pretzel cabin and something from the person who actually drew her name. There is no real way around this—even if Charlene manages to remove the other offending present without being noticed, the person who got Maria Jose's name is going to know something's up. So Charlene has decided that Maria Jose will just get two presents, and everyone will think it's a little mistake, and only Charlene and maybe Maria Jose will know what's true.

The mega-bookstore seems a good place to get Jerry's present. Once Charlene walked by his cubicle and saw him reading a book under his keyboard tray. Sometimes he leaves the lunchroom early, a book under his arm. She is never close enough to Jerry to see the title of what he's reading, so she walks up and down the aisles of the huge store, hoping something will jump out at her.

Wandering into the cookbook section, Charlene forgets all about Jerry and his present. There is a section on Latin American cuisine, and two books just on Salvadorean food. She pours over the pictures of pupusas and imagines slapping the tortillas between her palms over a hot grill while Maria Jose takes orders and charms the customers. At night—sweat drying on the back of their necks, tired down to the bone—they lock up the shop and walk home down the dirt road, back to their little house with the stream out back.

On her way up to pay for the cookbooks, Charlene passes a display of day planners and picks one up in maroon. That's the right present for Jerry—it's useful without saying much. She doesn't want to give him anything too intimate.

The roof takes hours, but it is soothing work. Charlene hums "Feliz Navidad" to herself as she carefully glues each pretzel stick to the gingerbread roof. Slowly the lines of pretzels begin to look like logs, and Charlene is pleased. She pauses to wipe off her fingertips, sticky with icing and pretzel dust.

The end of the pretzel cabin project is in sight. Charlene doesn't need the index cards anymore; she knows where to go from here. But first, she needs to finish this part, her favourite part: lining up the pretzel logs, side by side, watching the roof grow into something. Imagining Maria Jose leaning down to admire the perfectly aligned pretzel logs and reaching out to run her finger along the tip of the roof.

It never snows in El Salvador. Charlene makes the lawn out of green candies, mixing up the different kinds, Skittles beside jelly beans, for artistic effect. She stretches and admires her work. The lawn and roof look perfect. She glues a little plastic dog out front and behind him leaves a few melted chocolate chips, for realism. She traces the shapes of windows and uses sticks of gum for shutters. She mixes up different colours of icing and pipes on window boxes full of flowers. Finally, she melts the blue Jolly Ranchers in a saucepan on the stove, stirring until the hard squares are liquid and the pot smells like sky. Out back, behind the cabin, she spreads the blue goo into a stream that trickles to the edge of the tinfoil base. Charlene imagines it leading to the next cabin and the one after that, all of them connected by the thin, sweet stream.

When she finishes the back lawn, adding green banks alongside the candy stream, it is early in the morning. She pipes icing into an *M* and a *J* on one corner of the tinfoil base. Then she wraps Jerry's day planner in green tissue paper and attaches his name to the top. There is just enough time for the last of the details to dry completely while Charlene gets ready for work and the Christmas exchange and Maria Jose.

She takes a taxi to work to keep the pretzel cabin safe. The taxi driver glances back when she opens the door and gently slides the cabin over to its own seat before getting in and giving him the address of her office.

"Nice house. You make that?" he says, looking at her in the mirror.

Charlene nods and is glad when he doesn't say anything else, only looks over his shoulder and pulls out into the traffic. The darkness is just beginning to lift, the sky shifting to grey, backlit with shades of pink.

As planned, Charlene is the first to arrive at the office. She flicks on the light switch with her elbow and carries the pretzel cabin past the other empty cubicles to her own. Putting the cabin behind a stack of files where it will not be seen by Roberta or Tina or anyone else, she lines up her pens and wonders how she is going to manage to wait until lunchtime.

All morning people have been going in and out of the lunchroom. Charlene is waiting for the right moment to carry the pretzel cabin to the table of presents without being noticed. While she waits, she keeps peering over the pile of files to check on the cabin. Somehow not even one log has fallen off the roof, a real danger according to the internet. She hears Maria Jose's laugh, and the greyhounds do their flips inside her. She looks to see where the laugh is coming from. Maria Jose and Jerry are standing near the door of the lunchroom. Their heads are close together, and their voices are too quiet to hear, but Charlene watches Jerry's lips say *thank you*.

He has tissue paper in one hand, and a snow globe is sitting on top of it. He shakes it, and the flakes swirl around. When they settle, Charlene can see a little house inside the snow globe. A cabin.

Cyanide Necklace

DURING THE WAR, MY GRANDFATHER HAD TO WEAR A CYANIDE necklace. He was a wireless operator and had all of this information in his head that he couldn't let the Germans get a hold of, no matter what. He was told to swallow the cyanide pill around his neck if he was ever captured.

Once, he saw his friend decapitated by a trip wire, his head sliced clean off, right at the neck. He wrote letters home from Holland but not about decapitations and cyanide necklaces. The army wouldn't have let that kind of letter get out, and he didn't want to worry his mother.

What Vern Did

THE WHOLE TRIP HAD BEEN A BUST, ANYWAY, VERN DECIDED AS he stood in the aisle of the airplane waiting for people to move towards the exit.

Vern's prostate had been acting up this time, and between that and his upset stomach (probably from that shrimp off the buffet the second night), he seemed to have spent most of his time looking for a bathroom. As much as he loved Cuba, the toilets were garbage. Half the time no toilet paper at all, or paper so thin you could see your hand through it.

Usually Vern enjoyed these trips. He'd been going two or three times a year since retirement, and he looked forward to it every time. Even went to the tanning beds beforehand so he wouldn't look like a marshmallow with Q-tips for legs strolling down the beach.

Sometimes he got a girl, but with his body acting up this time, he didn't want to risk it. It was starting to look like things were about done in that department. Last time, the girl he got had to be at least fifty, and she moved like it, too. Not that he was one to talk, obviously, but the last thing he wanted was pussy that made him feel old.

He was glad his ex-wives weren't around to see this development. Lorraine especially would have a field day.

It wasn't that he hadn't loved Lorraine. Gemma and Aurelia too. He'd loved them all, but that was a separate thing. The girls were like dessert. You didn't need dessert with every meal, but when you did want it, more roast beef or an extra plate of salad wasn't going to cut it.

The first time Lorraine caught him, she had gone out to the car after he came home from work. Vern thought she was just getting something out of the garage until he heard the door of the sedan slam. Maurice, Lorraine's orange cat, jumped and fled upstairs.

"It smells like cigarettes in the car," Lorraine said from the doorway. She was blocking the exit.

"That was me. Sorry, honey."

"Huh."

Lorraine's short hair was sticking up in all directions. Her lips were pinched tight, and her eyebrows went up.

"That's interesting. Because I can also smell that same perfume your sister used to wear. Before she died." Lorraine was almost whispering.

Vern thought fast. Nostalgia? But Lorraine's features were getting squinty and pointy, and when she stomped out, her footsteps thunked like dropped bricks.

Now Aurelia, she was always making a big deal out of little things. If he forgot to lock the sliding door before bed, she acted like it was the Cuban Missile Crisis. If he dared to work late, they'd be locked in a standoff, the house in a vice of sexless silence—which didn't help things, obviously. She was a knockout, though, that Aurelia. Black curls down to her tits. Before they were married, when he was still with Lorraine, she'd come out of the bathroom at the Travelodge, and just looking at her got him hard.

Gemma wasn't the bombshell Aurelia was, but she was the one that stuck in his teeth a bit. She wanted kids but stayed with him when he refused to get his vasectomy reversed. In return, he pretended to listen to her adoption talk until it petered out after a year or so of his "We can talk about it"s and "Let me sleep on it some more"s.

Gemma never nagged him to get home earlier, and she gave this small, sexy gasp when she came. She was a little thicker than most of the other girls, and when she was tired or concentrating, one of her eyes wandered. It was hard not to think of a cat's-eye marble rolling around on her face.

Even Gemma had her limit, though. Took Vern a few years to figure out what it was—turns out coming home to two girls in the house, that was her limit. And that was the end of things with Gemma.

The line wasn't moving, and Vern had to piss. Aurelia would definitely have made a scene by now, if she'd been here. First just sighing loudly as if she could blow the line forward with one big breath. When that didn't work, she'd start complaining to him, loudly, about this terrible airline and its lazy staff and how she was going to get a new travel agent as soon as they got out of here. Then, finally, she'd start calling out something like, "Who is the manager here?" until the pilot came out and threw bags of pretzels at her until she shut up or, more likely, started throwing them back at him and swearing in Portuguese. Vern smiled.

The girl next to him was a curvy thing with blue toenails. She was in a middle seat, and her husband was beside the window, staring out at the snow blowing across the tarmac. The aisle seat was empty. The girl waggled her leg. Vern was still in his sandals, too, always changed them in the airport at the very last minute, holding on to the trip like a handful of sand falling through his fingers. The polish on the girl's big toe was chipped away, nearly gone like she'd been picking at it.

Vern shifted his feet. Somebody was pressing a can of soup against his bladder. The curvy girl nuzzled her husband's shoulder like she could have been wiping her nose on his sleeve, but she probably wasn't. The husband kept looking outside and patted her knee. The girl pulled out the inflight magazine and flipped through it too quickly to be reading anything. Aurelia used to flip through magazines like that when she was about to explode—since then he had always associated the sound of those perfumey, glossy pages rubbing together with a woman's rage. This trip, he'd been glad to see so many girls on the beach with those computer books, the ones that lit up white. Seeing a girl looking at a screen like that didn't remind him of anything.

With Lorraine, he wouldn't have been in this line at all. Maurice hated flying, she said, so she never went anywhere even when Vern invited her. Which he did from time to time, especially at the beginning. It wouldn't have been very hard to get her sister to sit with the cat. The first few times, Vern suggested that, but she just shrugged and didn't call her sister and pretty soon he stopped asking. After Lorraine left, Vern kept finding orange hairs everywhere, for months—in a teacup, on a suit he never wore, in his shaving cream. Like Maurice was getting the last word.

The curvy girl had a long black dress on. When she bent down to get something out of her purse, he could see the tops of her white tits where the tan stopped. She straightened up and leaned against the husband and reached her hand into his lap. As Vern watched, she rubbed him, slowly, looking out the window too. But the husband just sighed and shifted in his seat, took her hand out of his lap and put it back in her own. Vern looked away.

"But I like you curvy," Vern had said through the bathroom door. Gemma was being uncharacteristically dramatic.

"No you don't. Just leave me alone."

The truth was Gemma was more thick than curvy, but "I like you thick" didn't sound good in his head, and he had a feeling that wouldn't help the situation any. Eventually he just left her there and went to the Christmas party alone.

By the time he got there, everybody was kind of drunk. Asha and Jane were moving around the empty dance floor in dirty bare feet. Jane had this long dress on that she lifted up when she twirled, her elbows sticking out in points. She danced over to Vern and pulled him over to Asha, who took his hand too, and Vern hated dancing but stayed anyway.

Later he came out of the bathroom, and Jane was waiting for him. Her face was red, and her eyes were wet and glassy, but she was sexy, standing there with one elbow sticking out, handful of fabric in her fist, showing him that tanned, tight calf. He pulled her out of the light. There was too much cloth to get through, so he touched her through the dress, swirling his fingers over her clit until she came. She moaned into his mouth and reached for him.

When he got home from the party, the bathroom was dark and empty. Gemma was asleep. Vern washed his hands again to get the last bit of Jane off him. When he got into bed, Gemma sighed in her sleep and turned toward him.

Vern stuck his head out to the side to see what was happening, but nobody was moving. They were all just standing there, holding bags. Sighing and muttering and blocking his way out. The bathroom was way at the back of the plane, and there was no way he was going to be able to get back there now. The curvy girl was back at the magazine, whipping through the pages. Vern's bladder ached. He was old, sure, but not old enough for pissing himself to be okay.

He took a step to the left and unzipped. A whoosh of relief. The piss hit the back of the aisle seat's tray table and dripped down into the pocket. He stared straight ahead so he couldn't see if he was accidentally splashing the curvy girl's foot with its picked-away polish. He hoped not. He wouldn't have minded hitting the magazine, but it was well out of range of the dribble of piss.

The girl looked over at him just as he was zipping up. She glanced from his crotch to his face, and her eyes flickered surprise and something else he'd never seen on a woman's face before, something he couldn't put his finger on. She leaned over and whispered to her husband. Vern stared ahead, at the back of the man standing ahead of him, and pretended nothing had happened. Out of the corner of his eye, he saw the husband lean over the girl and check out the back of the seat.

"No way," he said.

"Can't you see it?" she hissed.

"Yeah, there's definitely something dripping there. We should tell someone."

"No," the curvy girl whispered. "I don't want to embarrass him. He's an old man."

And Vern knew that what he had seen in the girl's face was

worse than the fury he saw when Aurelia threw him out, worse than that look Lorraine got, all squinty and pointy. Worse than Gemma's face when she realized he was never going to have a kid with her. That look was worse even than pissing himself on an airplane, and it was something he didn't want to see, not ever again.

Dispatched

WHEN WE HEARD THE CALL COME OVER THE RADIO, WE THOUGHT the dispatcher must have been joking. I wanted to skip the call in case it really was a joke and then we would all look like idiots. But Reyes is a by-the-book kind of guy, so he flipped on the lights and then the siren and off we went.

We arrived at the scene of the disturbance just after 1:00 a.m. I tried to see in the windows while Reyes knocked on the door and called, "Hello? Police!" I couldn't see anything inside but a bit of light from a lamp in the corner. Reyes knocked again, and the door opened, and the couple came out on the porch.

The woman had dip on her forehead and arms, and her hair was full of chips. The man had crumbs all down his front and dip in his beard and hair. I covered my mouth so they wouldn't see me laugh, but Reyes is always professional.

"What was the dispute about?" he asked them, notepad out and ready.

"Only one beer left," the woman mumbled, pulling chips out of her hair.

Rebound in the Round

THERE WAS A BIG STREET PARTY ON THE NEXT BLOCK A WEEK OR so after we moved in. Everything was still in boxes, and I wanted to stay home and get things set up. But Jim said we should definitely go to try and meet the neighbours and fit in. He didn't say "fit in," but that's what he meant.

At the block party, I was in line for the potato salad when someone tapped me on the shoulder. She was a slim, pretty lady, the colour of a pale clementine.

"Hi there. Haven't seen you at one of these things before."

"We're new to the neighbourhood."

"Oh yeah? Where do you live?"

I told her the name of our street.

"Oh, Rebound in the Round. Nice trees over there."

"What?"

"Oh, sorry. You married?"

"Yeah."

Jim was standing close to the barbecue with some other guys, beer in his hand.

Jim is tall and handsome in a way that is non-threatening. His nose turns up a little. His hair used to be blond, but it's mostly grey now. He keeps it shorter than I would like, but you can't make Jim do things he doesn't want to do. When all of our city friends started getting married, the women would talk about what they needed to change about their husbands—more gym, less work, more help with the kids, less of the video games, more sex, or less. But Jim is stubborn. I figured there was no changing him, so I took him as is. He must have done the same thing, and so far we've been lucky because our flaws haven't been intolerable enough to fracture us.

I pointed him out to Orangey. Her perfect eyebrows raised, just for a second.

"First marriage?"

That seemed like a weird question to ask somebody when you haven't exchanged names yet. I guess Orangey must have seen that on my face because she said sorry and told me her name.

"Rhonda," I said.

"So is it?"

"What?"

"Your first marriage?"

"Yep."

"Well, that's a first. See, it's called Rebound in the Round (or some of the less educated types call it the Rebound Compound) because everybody there's on marriage number two. At least."

"The realtor didn't mention that," I said, trying to laugh it off.

"No, she wouldn't. But I wouldn't worry about it," Orangey said. "We should just get a new nickname for your street."

Shedding a nickname is harder than losing weight. I remember an overweight kid we used to call Smalls in grade school. He was the only kid we called anything other than his name. He went to a different high school, so I don't know if he ever managed to get rid of the weight or the nickname. I didn't mention any of this to Orangey, though.

The line for the potato salad was barely moving. They love their carbs in the suburbs, I imagined telling Jim later, and pictured the gentle look he always gives me when I'm being mean.

"What street do you live on?" I asked her.

She pointed behind the barbecuing men.

"Cherry Street."

"What do people call it?"

"Just Cherry Street."

"Nobody calls it Virgin Territory?"

Orangey tipped her head to one side like I was a puzzle she was trying to figure out. She didn't laugh.

"You got kids?" Orangey asked after we'd both plunked scoops of food on our plates and were standing around trying to eat and talk. When Jim and I were in our twenties and early thirties, people would ask us about kids all the time. I used to give long elaborate answers about being happy with the life we had or sometimes I'd make a joke about my broken biological clock. Sometimes I'd just keep talking until the asker looked pained and I trailed off. But when Orangey asked, I was closing in on forty, and people didn't ask as often anymore. When they did, I had finally learned to keep it simple.

"Nope," I told Orangey.

"You're lucky. If we didn't have the kids, I'd be living on Rebound in the Round myself."

She rolled her eyes in the direction of the ice-cream truck parked at the curb. "See that one?" she said, like we were peering under a mattress, looking for bedbugs.

There was a thin, young guy with a raggedy beard paying for a popsicle, and behind him was a square-shaped man without much hair, dog leash looped over his wrist attached to a little rust-coloured dog. The square man was standing on his tiptoes and squinting at the truck's menu. The dog was yapping and trying to pull in the opposite direction.

"The man with the dog?"

"Yeah, that's Dave." Orangey rolled her eyes again. "Kids are over with my sister somewhere," she said, gesturing behind herself without turning to look.

That night, I told Jim about Rebound in the Round.

"I think I like Rebound Compound better. Not so elitist."

I kind of agreed with him.

"Don't you think it's weird, though? Not one original marriage on the block?"

"The houses all look the same. Why should the marriages

be different?"

He moved to the other side of the sectional and stretched out.

"Do you think it's bad luck?"

"I doubt it," he said, picking up the remote.

It was Jim's idea to have a party for the cul-de-sac.

"You're all about meeting the neighbours these days, aren't you?"

"It'd be nice, I think, no?"

Jim has always been better at being around people. When we hold each other's hands at the edge of a party, it's always mine that's clammy. On vacation, he chats with the person next to him on the airplane while I read. When we walk by the lake, he goes straight up to strangers and asks them what they're fishing for. At the end of a trip once, he disappeared into the airport throng while I waited with our stuff at the gate. When he came back, grinning, he handed me a plastic bag with something soft in it. When I opened it, I glared at him. The t-shirt said, *All I care about is food and avoiding people.* He leaned over and kissed me on the forehead, and we both started laughing.

"I saw that in a store near the food court. Do you like it?"

"I hate it," I said and kissed him.

When he asked me what I thought of his idea to have the party, I said the same thing, but I didn't kiss him.

"I'll make my lasagna, and we can get a bunch of snack foods. You won't have to cook anything."

"Will I have to clean up?"

"Nope. I'll do everything. All you have to do is be there." Jim smiled and the sides of his eyes got crinkly, and I couldn't think of a decent reason to say no.

On the day of the party, I kept dragging the Swiffer around the kitchen and every part of the house that wasn't carpeted.

"I think it's probably clean, honey," Jim said, sliding the second lasagna into the oven.

"What time are they coming again?"

"Seven," Jim said, as if I hadn't asked him four times already.

"Who did we invite?"

"Everybody on Rebound Compound, the realtor, those guys I met at the barbecue and their wives, and Orangey and her husband."

I thought about Dave in line at the ice-cream truck and how he looked like an ant that had fallen into a jar of honey.

"I hope you didn't call her Orangey when you invited her!"

Jim laughed. He pulled bottles out of a liquor-store box and slid a bottle of white wine into the freezer behind me.

"You always forget that's in there. It's going to explode. Don't forget this time."

"Good tip," Jim said, and patted my butt as he moved around me.

Except for the realtor, everybody at the party kind of looked like everybody else. I kept mixing the husbands up.

"Here's your whiskey," I said, handing one what I thought he'd ordered.

"Oh, thanks, but I can't stomach whiskey." The husband rubbed his round stomach to demonstrate in a way that made my own stomach feel out of sorts.

"Of course. I'll bring you a Coke," I said, figuring his stomach problem was code for drinking problem.

"Put some rum in it, will you?"

I brought the whiskey to a different husband.

"Thanks, but I'm a beer guy," he said.

After I brought the rum to the first husband and the beer to the second husband, I drank the whiskey myself in the kitchen and gave up on drink orders.

Our realtor, Sinead, seemed to know everybody at the party already. She had dark hair that seemed to get more lush and full and luxurious every time she ran her hands through it, which was a lot. And that accent—when she spoke it sounded like a mourning dove, musical in a way that could be interpreted as haunting or hopeful depending on how you were feeling when you heard it.

Sinead was telling a story about an open house gone wrong.

"From outside, it looked ready. The lawn was cut close, and there were planters full of purple flowers at the entranceway, like the stager had suggested. But inside, everything was a mess. The family hadn't cleaned anything up, and I didn't have time to tidy before people started arriving. There was peanut butter all over everything, the kitchen, even the walls in the entranceway. Chip bags crumpled up and thrown down on the carpet like it was a landfill site or a bus-station parking lot. Can you believe it?"

Her laugh rippled out into the room. One or two husbands were standing closer to her than they needed to. One of them was Dave. He was leaning in to listen and laughing when Sinead laughed, but his was kind of wheezy.

Orangey sidled up to where I was, leaning against a wall at the edge of the party.

"She's something, isn't she?"

I looked at her to see what kind of something she meant. She was looking at Sinead, but it wasn't jealous or hostile. It was like she didn't even see Dave there, or if she did, he didn't really matter at all.

People started drinking more. Eventually Sinead left, which was okay because some of the guests were starting to get slurry, and I was figuring somebody was either going to paw at her or try to tear her head off, and that was probably not the impression Jim wanted us to make on the neighbourhood. Besides, I liked Sinead. Even though Orangey said that she was the one that turned the cul-de-sac into the Rebound Compound in the first place.

"She hand-picked everybody who lives on this street. She's got her eye on the husbands, and she knows they're vulnerable, so she gathered them all up here in one place. Easy pickings," Orangey said, draining her glass as she walked away. That seemed off to me. For starters, besides Jim, none of the husbands were very good looking or, from what I could tell, very interesting. And even Jim was a step down for Sinead.

The other thing was, what did "vulnerable" mean? Because

they had been through divorces or because they were men?

Iris somebody-or-other came over to me to say goodbye. Her face was puffy and pink from booze, but the rest of her was pipe-cleaner thin. Next to her, I felt like a lumpy futon.

"You should come to my yoga class sometime," she said as she backed down the walk.

"Maybe," I said, shutting the door as she was still waving.

I was glad Jim was busy talking to some people in the kitchen, so I didn't have to see that gentle look.

I started to go into the kitchen to make sure Jim had taken the bottle of wine out of the freezer.

Orangey was holding a plastic bag while Jim put shards of glass into it. I backed up and stood just outside the entranceway, out of their sightline, but I could see them.

"We can't let Rhonda see that I forgot to take this out again," Jim said. I smiled.

Orangey stepped closer to him, reached around, and touched the small of his back with a manicured hand. She was looking at him with Dave's Sinead expression. My jaw and stomach clenched.

"I won't say a word," Orangey said.

Jim reached behind himself, peeled her hand off his back, and put it down by her side. He didn't say anything, just shook his head no, and turned and walked out of the kitchen. I reached out and grabbed his hand. He saw me then, and I pulled him to me and hugged him around his middle, breathing in his smell of detergent and deodorant, soap and skin.

"You were right about the bottle."

"Yep," I said, hugging him tighter.

A few weeks later, I did end up going to yoga with Iris. She showed up at my door, green designer mat under her arm, and I wasn't busy and I couldn't think of an excuse fast enough, so I went with her. It was at the community centre on Cherry Street, and we walked there, which no one does in the suburbs, so it made me like Iris a bit more.

"So how did people start calling our street Rebound in the Round?" I asked Iris.

She looked confused.

"What?"

"Okay Rebound Compound then," I said, taking a guess.

"That's a cute name. What does it mean?"

"You've never heard that before?"

"You made it up, right? It's cute," Iris said, folding her fingers in half to check out her nails, painted peach.

"Everyone calls it that."

"Honey, I've lived here fourteen years, and I've never heard anybody say that before," she said, waving at somebody I couldn't see. When I turned, Dave and the little rust dog were coming over to us.

"Lovely to see you two ladies," Dave said, but he was talking to Iris, his eyes flicking to the strip of flat stomach showing below her tank top.

"Good to see you, Dave. Say hello to your wife for me," she said as she walked away.

"I don't know how that guy stays married," she said, pulling open the door to the community centre with her wiry arm. I looked back and Dave was standing still, watching Iris as the little dog pulled, trying to get away.

Family

THE LITTLE BOY CRAWLED UNDER THE HAMMOCK AND FLIPPED his uncle's girlfriend out of it and onto the grass. She put on her sunglasses so he wouldn't see she was starting to cry.

Later, after board games, he pushed her in the stomach. Hard. She tried not to be bothered and went to look for her sunglasses. The boy's mother noticed and gave him a timeout.

"You can't do that. You can't hurt her," the mother scolded.

The little boy said: "What? She's in my family."

Everything Inside

MOST PEOPLE HAVEN'T COME BACK, AND SOME SAY THEY WON'T.
We didn't know what else to do. We stayed with George's parents
for a while, in Tallahassee, but in their tiny place, we were all on
top of each other. We're getting older, not too far from fifty now,
and they're old folks. It wasn't easy. George's mom started off the
day with a bite to her, and his dad looked down at his hands a lot,
more than usual, like there was something in those old, rough
fingers that would help him get us out.

We couldn't stand it, anyway, not being home. Even though
the city doesn't look like ours anymore. It seems like there's never
sun, though of course there must be, but since we've been back,
it feels like the sky is just different versions of grey. Light grey
during the day, and at night, black. The electricity's still out, so
we've got a lantern and candles for outside and two flashlights for
inside the tent. We don't go out at night, either of us. Sometimes
we hear shots or yelling, and George grips my hand. There's a little
bell attached to the zipper on our tent, so if anybody tries to get in
again, we'll hear it.

Right now, there is no sound inside the tent. Outside is pretty
quiet too, except for a cat making noise somewhere close by. Cars
from the highway. Before, we couldn't even hear the highway from
here, but nothing is the same since the storm. The Superdome
looms over that highway, those missing panels leaving big jack-o-
lantern gaps in the shell.

It's early, probably before six. George's gone out already, biking around town like he does every morning now. I tell him not to, that it'll just make him feel worse, but he says he has to. When he comes back later in the day, we sit in lawn chairs outside the tent, and he leans towards me till I can smell the beer on him, and he tells me what he saw that day:

On top of a pile of bricks, enough to fill three dump trucks, a wood sign painted red: "Looters will be shot."

A roof squished in, bent in the middle like a giant put his fist through it. Sand spilling out from what could have been a bedroom or a kitchen.

Concrete steps leading to nowhere, the house gone.

Everywhere, on our street too: red Xs and death tolls spray-painted on boarded up windows. Dates that the houses were checked for corpses, sometimes weeks after the storm hit.

A yellow school bus, half sunk in the dirt so just its end was sticking up.

The Common Ground clothing tent where people mill around looking for things that might fit them. Outside of it, a volunteer sorting through a mountain of cloth.

A stuffed lion, smeared with mud, lying on its back in the road. One ear missing.

The balconies in the French Quarter with their green, lush plants dangling down towards the street.

From what he tells me about what he sees, I'm surprised George isn't drinking more than he is. I don't usually leave the yard. I don't want to see any of it.

Our house is rubble. I've already picked through it to see if anything was left to save, and we've got what we could find in big plastic boxes beside the tent. There wasn't much: a sweater I used to like, some dishes and things from the kitchen, a few books, some extra shoes for both of us. And, thank God, a few photos and our important papers and my mother's earrings. They were in a strongbox. Those are with us in the tent.

Every morning, George leaves a bottle of water beside our air mattress for me. And by the flap of the tent, he leaves the bucket, so I don't have to go outside before I'm ready to. He's still a sweet man, and I hope this storm won't do to him what it did to our fridge.

George and a friend of his managed to get the fridge out to the curb when we first got back. They told us not to open the fridges, that it wasn't safe. They told us to tape them shut and stay away from them. I've thought a lot about what was in that fridge when the storm hit. I made a list of everything I could remember. Sometimes when I look at my list, I think I can smell what was in there like it's not even rotten: leftover chili, milk, yoghurt, cabbage, blueberries, even carrots, which are harder to smell. But after two months, I'm pretty sure that even the hardiest foods in there—mustard, maybe even the beef jerky—are moving with maggots. I stay away from the fridge.

We cook over a hibachi in the yard. George brings home fresh things sometimes, and we open cans a lot. I salvaged a decent pot from our house, and that's been working well enough.

Cooking is manageable, but I hate not being able to go to the bathroom properly. There are a few of those blue portable toilets set up on our street. Some agency brought them by. It was nice of them, I guess, but the toilets are disgusting. I can't stand going in there. As soon as you open the door, it smells like when we walked down the subway steps in New York that time. It smells like homeless people in those blue toilets. I'm afraid of what will crawl up when I'm sitting there. Sometimes there is brown on the walls. I try to do what I have to outside, at the back of our yard.

Yesterday I was finishing up, at the back of our yard, when I heard somebody call out a hello. It was the neighbour who used to live behind us. I was glad I'd already pulled my pants up and was just kicking dirt over what I'd done when she called to me. I could pretend I'd been doing something else back there if she asked, which she didn't.

"That you, Miss Sharon?" she called.

Tammy looked thinner, and there was more grey showing through her black hair than I remembered. Her eyes were darker, too.

"It is. Didn't know you were back."

"I'm not. We're still in Mississippi at my sister's. I just drove in to see if I could save anything."

"Any luck?"

"Not much. The place is totally destroyed," Tammy said, waving behind her at her place.

I'd already seen it, every time I had to go, but I pretended like it was the first time I was looking.

The back of her house was ripped off, so you could see everything inside what had been her living room. Beige sofa blackened by mould. Smashed television, kicked in and lying on its side. A pile of boards that could have been a table. The carpet mostly gone, and the floor strewn with garbage and bricks and fabric.

"Doesn't look good," I said.

"Yours neither."

"No," I agreed.

"The front is a bit better, I guess," Tammy said. "The mailbox is still in one piece, for some reason."

"Is that right?" Our mailbox was long gone. George thought maybe he'd seen it on another street.

"Yeah. And you'll never believe it—we got mail."

"You did? Something from FEMA?"

Tammy snorted. "Hardly."

I waited.

"I open up the mailbox just now, and I get this," she said, holding up her hand and showing me a white envelope.

"What is it?"

"A fucking electricity bill," she said through tight teeth.

"You're kidding!"

"Nope. No electricity here since before the storm, right?"

"No," I said. "We're using flashlights and candles still."

"Right. And I don't even have a house to light up, even if the electricity was working. And the city sends me a goddamn bill."

She crumpled up the envelope, drew back her arm, and pitched the thing towards the back of her hollowed-out house. It didn't get far and landed in the mud a few feet in front of her. She kicked mud over it, splashing her sneakers and jeans, until the last bit of white disappeared.

The power was out the night I lost the second baby. I was further along this time, and we were hopeful, more hopeful than we should have been, I guess. The pain and wet woke me up. I sat up and tried to turn on the lamp, but it wasn't working. I felt around beside me, but George wasn't there. The screen on the clock radio was black.

I scribbled George a note in the darkness and left it on his pillow. I drove myself to the hospital, leaking out onto a towel. Our street was dark, and the next one over, but the power seemed to be on after that. Streetlight blazed into the car. I stared at the road so I wouldn't look down.

George was already crying when he came into the hospital room.

"I'm sorry, Sharon. Sorry. I should have been there."

He sat down in the chair beside me and put his head down on the bed. I smoothed his hair. He was breathing into the blanket, but I could still smell the booze.

He cried for a long time, like it was for both of us. I was sad too, but the sad felt far away, and I didn't really want to get closer to it. I stroked his hair, already turning grey then. The first time, he was the one touching my hair, telling me we'd try again. The second time, neither of us said anything.

These days, George is always home before it gets dark. I wonder if he ever thinks of that night, if that's why he comes home early, whether he's been drinking or not. Nearly fourteen years now, it's been, so maybe he isn't thinking about that at all. Maybe he comes home early because he is scared, more of what's inside him than what's in the city.

We'd only been back a few days when the man opened the tent. He did it softly and quietly, and George was snoring beside me, so I didn't even hear him until the tent was open. I didn't have my glasses on, and it was dark, so all I could see was a big fuzzy shape, rooting around the entrance to the tent. I screamed. Whoever it was might have been as scared as me because he backed out of the tent right away. But George was fast. He was up and out the tent after him, moving from dead sleep to chasing in what felt like seconds.

"Hey! HEY!" I could hear George yelling. There was a shuffling sound, grunting, and some kind of thud. Then there was a whack that made me feel sick. "George. George!" I screamed, crawling towards the tent flap.

"I'm okay, Sharon!" George yelled. "Stay inside! Stay inside the tent!" His voice sounded strange, wet and scared and fast.

Then his voice changed into a growl I'd never heard before.

"Get up, man. Get up and get the fuck out of here."

I didn't hear anything except George's voice saying that, over and over. Then I heard a groaning sound and some rustling and shuffling and then quiet. There was a chunk of time where nothing happened; I don't know how long it was. Then I heard George settle outside the tent on a lawn chair, heard the hiss and pop of a beer opening. I sat in the tent, hugging my knees and waiting for him to come back in, for a long time. A cat wailed. Cars whirred down the highway by the Superdome.

When George finally came back in, everything outside was quiet. I lay down next to him and touched his face, but without my glasses I couldn't tell what the wet was.

"George?" I said, softly so I wouldn't startle him.

"Everything's okay, Sharon," he said in a gentle voice and put his arms around me, and if it had been before everything, the babies and the storm and the man, I probably would have believed him.

Where's Edward?

JOSEPH'S MOTHER, AGNES, LIVED THE LAST FEW YEARS OF HER life in a nursing home. For a long time, both of her sons visited her every week. One week, when Agnes was ninety-three, Edward didn't show up.

"Where's Edward?" Agnes asked Joseph.

Joseph looked away.

"We haven't seen him lately," said Joseph's wife.

"Where is that little bugger?" Agnes asked the week after that.

"I don't know," said Joseph's wife.

Joseph's adult sons and their families came for a visit.

"Where is Edward?" she asked them. The ones who lied best stepped forward and said things: they'd seen him, or they hadn't.

Nobody had the heart to tell Agnes that Edward had died, so when she died herself at ninety-five, she thought she had one good son and one bad one because Joseph's wife said it was better to have a bad son than a dead one.

Windpipe

JEANNETTE SHUTS THE DOOR OF THE RENTAL AND DOESN'T bother to lock it. Before she turns away, she glances into the back seat. The pink cake box is sitting on the grey upholstery. Dammit, Paul. Her jaw tightens. How hard is it to bring a cake in? She bites down on her frustration—a jolt between her teeth, like cartilage in meat.

The grey sky is not bright enough for sunglasses, but too bright to see without squinting. Jeannette looks up at St. Elizabeth's. The roof of the church is the colour of rust. Behind the church is a chestnut tree, its green spiky fruit waiting to fall and be split. Flat green leaves spread out like splayed hands.

The concrete path leading to the church is cracked and breaking apart. Weeds push themselves up in the cracks. Some of them stretch up, and others droop towards the ground. A car growls on another road. Just to her left is a slight scrabbling: a fat squirrel is bellying through the grass towards the church. It changes its mind and heads in the opposite direction.

At the door to St. Elizabeth's, Jeannette stops and listens, but there is no sound from inside. No off-key choir at practice, no chanted creeds. She sighs with relief. She pulls open the thick, heavy door by its old iron ring. In the faded light, she smells the memory of incense and varnish on pews. She moves to the last pew on the left. When she was a kid, her family always sat in the back on the left. If another family was already sitting there, her father would ask them to move.

Jeannette was mortified then; now, she admires it, how her father took what he wanted instead of just slinking away to another spot for the sake of not making a scene.

The pew creaks as she sits down. She runs her hands over the smooth wood and looks up at the stained-glass windows. Coloured light filters in, slanting down to the floor. The grey light of outside is changed in here into lines of yellow, pools of blue. She stretches and leans on the back of the pew ahead of hers.

When she was little, she couldn't see anything from the back, but she could still hear. "And even if you can't see the altar, the priest can see you," her mother would whisper to her when she started fidgeting, flicking off her shoes and slouching down to rub her stocking feet across the hardwood floor, trying to cool them. Shouldn't the priest be paying attention to what he's doing up there? God can keep an eye on me for him. She didn't tell her mother this.

In the empty church, her view of the altar is unobstructed. It is a brown wood table under a cloth the soft white of sifted flour. The legs of the table look smooth, like you wouldn't catch your skin or get a splinter, even if you ran your hands up them the wrong way.

Jeannette stretches and leans back against the pew. She pulls her legs up underneath her and sits cross-legged, closes her eyes and breathes, slowly and deeply, into her belly as her yoga teacher taught her before she stopped going. She bends her elbows to bring her hands to her shoulders, pressing them down so they don't inch up to her ears. Then she brings her hands into her lap and lets them rest there. She stretches her jaw to untighten it. Inside the church, there is only quiet. Jeannette rests her neck against the back of the pew and concentrates on the in and out of her breath.

Sometimes, when Jeannette goes shopping in her neighbourhood, she stands in front of a suit store window for a while. The window is full of mannequin men with silvery skin. They are dressed sharply in navy blue and pin stripes, ties immaculately knotted at grey throats. Their lips are pursed, keeping things in. The mannequin men have nostrils, and

Jeannette wonders if they are shallow holes, scraped out for show, or whether the holes go right up into their fibreglass heads. She wonders how far they will go for the illusion of breath.

Paul used to pull her to him after sex. Turn her over and draw her close so they were curled beside each other like quotation marks. He always fell asleep first, his breathing heavy in her ear. She'd hold her breath to match it up with his, exhaling when he did, until she fell asleep too.

Last night, she got out of bed when he came to it.

"I think I want to get that cake for the boys started instead of waiting until the morning," she said. He shrugged and pulled the blankets up.

In the kitchen, Jeannette wiped her hand across the smooth, wooden island in the middle of the room. White specks wafted out into the still air. She wet a cloth at the sink and cleaned the surface. She pulled out the ingredients she needed and lined them up on the island: dry beside dry, wet beside wet. Flour, sugar, baking powder, cocoa, salt, semi-sweet chocolate. Eggs, oil, vanilla. Two mixing bowls, a whisk apiece. Baking pans, wire rack. Wooden spoons that knocked and echoed against the canister as she pulled them out. Everything she needed for her easiest birthday cake. Every time she makes this particular cake, she adds a secret ingredient, one only she knows about. Every cake has a different secret. Once she put a dash of thyme into the chocolate icing. Another time she buried one chocolate chip inside a pristine vanilla cake. This time she chose something the nephews would hate if they could taste it.

Jeannette pulled out three beets from the crisper. She scrubbed them and peeled their thick brown skins into the sink. She held them by their dark red-green hair and rinsed them again. The exposed beets were purple-red and dripping. She thunked them against the side of the sink and left them on the counter while she got the food processor from the shelf under the microwave.

She chopped up the beets on a wooden cutting board, staining it dark red. Her fingers were purpling, too, vegetable blood under her nails. She scooped up the chopped beets and dropped them into the basin of the food processor and plugged it in, smudging the cord with beet blood. She clicked the top shut and whirred the red into a smooth blur.

When the noise of the food processor stopped, the doorframe creaked behind her. Jeannette looked over her shoulder.

"What are you doing?" Paul said.

"What do you mean? I'm making the cake for your nephews. I told you that."

"Why are you putting beets in their cake?"

"To make it moist," Jeannette said.

Paul looked at her for a long time.

"Can't you put applesauce in it or something? Beets seem like kind of a weird thing."

"Do you want to make the cake?" Jeannette snapped.

Paul sighed.

"Never mind. I'm going back to bed."

He pushed himself off the doorframe and walked away.

Since the beets were no longer a secret, thanks to Paul, she needed something else. She moved through the kitchen, opening the crisper in the fridge, the cupboards above the stove. Her spice rack was full but nothing was right.

The plant on the windowsill needed water. A dusty leaf was next to it on the ledge. Jeannette picked it up, her red fingers rubbing the new secret ingredient clean.

It was very late by the time the cake was cooling on its wire rack. Jeannette took one of her cookbooks to the couch and read until she fell asleep.

When they pulled into the driveway for the twins' party, it sounded like there were a dozen other ten-year-old boys there, too. Shouting without words, then a "Hey! Asshole." A screech of laughter, a smash. A metallic clatter: something colliding with something else.

The smell of hot dogs, almost burned, drifted through Jeannette's open window. Her stomach turned.

"Smells good," Paul said.

"I'll be back in a bit," Jeannette said.

Paul frowned, green eyes squinting under greying eyebrows. "Do you have to?"

"Yes," she said.

They argued about it for a few minutes, out of habit.

"Do you have to go to that fucking church every single time we come out here?"

When Paul cursed he always sounded like a ten-year-old trying to be an adult.

"Yes," she said. "I like it there."

"Why? What's the big deal? You don't even go to church anymore, and it's not like you know anybody who's buried there."

Exactly. I don't know anybody there. It's peaceful. It doesn't have you and your family in it.

"It's peaceful. I like the quiet," she said.

"Our whole life is quiet!" Paul snapped.

Not quiet enough.

"Why don't you come in for one hot dog and then you can go?" he whined.

She shook her head.

"Hot dogs are difficult to get out of your windpipe if they get stuck," she said quietly.

"What?"

Nothing.

Paul rolled his eyes. "I think the boys know how to chew. They're ten. The whole point of coming out here is to see my family, and you're not even coming in."

He rubbed his face with one hand. His fingers were pink and slender, his nails long. He didn't look at her as he bent down, collecting presents from the floor of the car. He snagged a nail on some shiny purple paper, ripping the wrapping into a crooked scar. A yellow Lego box peeked through. It didn't seem like he noticed, but maybe he just didn't want her to mention his nails again.

She looked away. Paul hit the door shut with his hip. Once she reversed out of the driveway onto the road, she glanced back. He was already inside.

They used to hold hands a lot, his fingers threaded through her olive-skinned, rugged ones. Her nails were always short, for baking, and her hands never seemed as clean as his.

Sometimes there would be a sliver of chocolate pushed up against a cuticle or a bit of flour lingering on her wrist. She remembers lifting his pristine hand and pressing it to her mouth as they walked along lanes in the city, feeling her heart shift with love for him.

She's supposed to be watching her thoughts drift by like boats, and it isn't working today. Stewing isn't meditating, her yoga teacher used to say. Jeannette stands up, stretches, and leaves the church. She goes around back to the graveyard.

The lawn is lush and unruly, a few weeks overdue for a trim. Grave markers slope down like curved backs into the grass. They are mostly fish-coloured marble, overcooked salmon and the shimmery grey of caught trout. In front of one stone is a tipped-over plastic pot, dry soil spilling out and away from a shrivelled red geranium. Jeannette picks up the pot and scoops soil back in with her fingers, patting it gently around the flower. Browning petals drop off as she tries to put it back together. She gathers saliva in her mouth and spits into the pot, as much as she can, but when she touches the soil it is not even damp.

When she sits down, the heat of the stone soaks through her yoga pants to her skin. She pulls off her sneakers and socks, and the grass is cool and soothing against her feet. She leans against the grave marker. Breathes in and out for a few minutes, turns her face up to the grey sun.

Her stomach growls.

Jeannette gets back up and walks across the grass. When the ground turns to gravel, the sharp stones scrape the soles of her bare feet. She reaches the car and opens the back door.

Carefully, she pulls out the cake, balancing it in one hand as she closes the door with the other.

She carries the cake back up to the graveyard. There is a smudge of icing on top of the box. She bends over and licks the cardboard, the caramel buttercream deep and sweet.

She eats the whole cake with her hands, leaning against the warm stone. Her taste buds try to locate the beets, but they are nowhere to be found. The pureed leaf is invisible. She probably has icing on her chin, but there is no one to point it out. The cake is perfect, one of her best: moist and smooth, every bite balanced and complete. Paul always wants his cake with milk, like a little boy, but Jeannette prefers it this way: by itself. Whole.

Eggplant Baby

THE GROCERY STORE IS NOT THE MOST EXCITING PLACE TO WORK, but sometimes it's kind of funny. One of the funny things at the store is the signs. The best sign Martina ever saw was the one that said *Eggplant Baby* in a big, black font you could see from the next aisle over. She made a point to walk by there on her breaks so she could check to make sure it was still there. It stayed there for a few weeks, even after all the eggplant babies were sold, hanging forlorn in front of an empty shelf. *Eggplant Baby* made Martina think of the Barbapapas, the TV blobs that looked like coloured-in eights. Somebody else must have noticed the sign too because one day when she went into produce to check on it, there was a whole new batch of eggplants, lined up shiny and purple-black, and there was a sign that said *Baby Eggplant*, and that was the end of that funny thing.

Another funny thing is the stock boys. There are so many of them, and they all kind of look the same, and they are always standing around checking their phones. But they do it in the aisles, beside carts full of boxes meant for the shelves, so customers have to squeeze past them only to get to an empty shelf with a lying sign. The stock boys are mostly teenagers or in their early twenties, checking out the younger cashiers over the tops of their phones. The owners are hardly ever around, but when they are, the stock boys suddenly get very busy pulling cans out of boxes and guiding the carts back to the pen outside. But the rest of the time it's like they're getting paid to clog up the aisles.

Once a lady brought a frozen cake up to Martina with a scrunchy look on her face.

"I was trying to get a birthday cake for my husband ..."

Martina gave a customer his change and receipt, pushing the cash drawer shut as she turned to the cake lady.

"And I just want you to know that this cake is four months past its expiry date!"

The lady's face was all wrinkled up with disgust, like those stuffed dogs Martina's cousins had when she was a kid, their faces all folds and ripples.

"I'm so sorry. Let me take that for you. I'll let them know right away," Martina said, taking the cake and putting it beside her register. The lady's face softened and smoothed out a little.

"I know it's not your fault, dear. Thanks for taking care of it," she said, pulling up the strap of her purse and walking elegantly out of the store. Martina wondered why cake lady was shopping at this store when she could probably afford to go to the fancy organic gourmet place that everybody at the store calls Whole Paycheck.

"Frozen foods, cash three please. Frozen foods, cash three," she said into the intercom and turned to the next customer. But nobody came. At the end of Martina's shift, the cake was still sitting there. All the other girls were busy cashing out by then, and there were no stock boys in sight, so she slipped the expired cake into one of the yellow plastic bags next to the till. It tasted a little off, sure, but a cake was a cake, so Martina and her mother finished it while watching *The Golden Girls*. Martina tried to pretend it was fresh cheesecake and they were sitting around a kitchen table in sunny Florida, but it was hard to forget that she was just eating old carrot cake.

Martina and her mother like to think of themselves as Dorothy and Sophia. Sometimes Martina's mother will start a sentence with "Picture it ...," and Martina rolls her eyes just like Dorothy would, and they both laugh. Of course, Toronto is not Miami at any time of year, and Martina is not tall and willowy like Dorothy. She also prefers to think she has better taste in clothes. Martina's mother is not pocket-size like Sophia, and she doesn't go out to bet on horses or meet men in parks. In fact, she doesn't go out much at all. If they had a lanai, she might go out on that, but all they have is a fire escape and the door is too heavy for either of them to open.

Watching *The Golden Girls* with her mother is only one of Martina's routines. At the end of a shift, she always scoops up any extra grocery receipts lying around near the conveyor belts at the checkout. If anyone asks, she'll say she's just tidying up. But no one does, and she stuffs the receipts into the pocket of her fleece as she pushes the automatic door that never works and goes out into the night.

When she gets home, she takes the receipts into her room and puts them under her pillow before she gets out of her uniform and into her robe. Most evenings, Martina hangs out with her mother and watches TV and knits another scarf. Sometimes she goes to the movies with her friend Sandra from work or goes out to a bar around the corner with some of the other older girls. Whatever she's doing, she always ends up alone in her room at the end of the night, and every night her ritual is exactly the same.

Martina gathers her supplies—scrapbook, glue, and pencil case from the drawer and receipts from under the pillow—and sits at her desk. She used to do her homework at this same desk when she was little. She turns to a clean page in the scrapbook and dates it. Then she uncaps the gluestick, smears the glue over the backs of that day's receipts, and smooths them onto the page. When the receipts are secured, she reads every word, whispering them out loud to herself like a prayer.

Sometimes the electronic shorthand makes no sense. Why would organic spinach be shortened to *ORG SPINACH*? Once in a while, she will come across something she doesn't recognize— what the hell is *MASSERIE OIL*? Sounds like something Blanche would buy—and she underlines it in black marker to remind herself to ask one of the other girls what it means.

By now she recognizes a lot of the items, and she takes care to read out the proper names to herself. She likes the way the quiet words sound in her little room. She finds *WW BRD WHOLE WHT* and whispers, "Weight Watchers Bread Whole Wheat." She knows that *PC CHDR MARBLE* is cheese slices and that, for some reason, peanut-butter chocolate cookies ring through as *PB CHCLATE COKIE*. This is pretty funny; she is happy the day she finds the *cokie*. But what she's really looking for is eggplant baby.

Martina has promised herself that the day she finds *BBY EGGPLNT* on a receipt, she is going to quit her job. Martina is a little bit afraid that if she doesn't make herself leave the store, she never will, and when she retires, she will have only ever done this one thing in this one place, and that is much more depressing than eating expired carrot cake without a lanai.

Martina's mother is always talking about signs. She got married in May, and it snowed that weekend for the first time in three decades. For thirteen years, her mother has said, "That snow was a sign we never should have gotten married" every time her dead husband comes up in conversation. She was probably saying it before he died, too, but just not to Martina.

Her friend Sandra believes in signs too, but only if they are pointed out by her psychic. She's not great at paying attention to actual signs, so Martina is kind of glad she lost her licence, and now they just take the subway to the movies. Sandra is Blanche without the shoulder pads. She calls herself sexually free. Martina's mother would call her a slut if she knew about Sandra's adventures with various stock boys. But Martina is amazed by her friend. On Sandra's break, she'll go up to the ones that smoke outside, and she might ask them for a cigarette or she might just stand there and chat with them. Martina stays inside and watches through the glass. Sandra laughs and pushes them on the arm sometimes, and they never roll their eyes when she walks away. Sometimes they look at her like she's a piece of cheesecake. Sandra comes back inside and sways over to the till, smiling and confident. If there's a new boy, as there usually is, she might have his phone number on a receipt that she waves in the air before pocketing. Martina wishes she could check the other side of the receipt for eggplant baby, but she wants to keep her project secret.

One afternoon, Martina goes into work and sees a new stock

boy. She notices him right away because he's a stock man, really. He looks like he's in his forties too, but older than she is, and he's kind of thick in his legs and middle. A stocky man. He has a lot of hair, wavy and dyed a strange colour, bluish black. Martina thinks it is beautiful. He smiles at her as she passes the mound of bananas. His eyes are the same blue as Blanche's. She smiles back. It's pretty quiet in the store until late afternoon, so Martina is able to keep an eye on the new stock man from her cash. He smiles a lot at people, customers and staff, women and men, everybody. And he has a way of smiling at people that isn't sleazy or sarcastic like the boys. After a few hours of stocking and smiling, it's time for his fifteen-minute. He doesn't go outside or into the break room or down the street to do errands. Instead he slowly walks around produce, looking at everything. She sees him straighten out the bags of carrots. He examines the tomatoes, picks one up and wipes something off it with his sleeve before putting it carefully back. He is leaning over the zucchini when Sandra sidles up to Martina's cash.

"That's the new guy, eh? What a weirdo."

"Hmm."

"Like why would you spend your break hanging around in produce looking at vegetables? He can do that all day."

"Who knows?" says Martina, hoping this will be enough of a response to make Sandra stop and change the subject.

It isn't.

"Also if I'm working here when I'm fifty ..."

Martina turns away from produce and looks at Sandra.

"I mean, not you obviously, you're so young still ..."

Sandra fidgets and a splotch of red shows up on her neck.

"I mean, it's different for stock boys anyway; I mean it says right in the name ..."

Sandra fiddles with her necklace and looks so uncomfortable that Martina lets her off the hook.

"It's okay. I know what you meant. Speaking of stock boys, any gossip?"

By the time Sandra's given her the highlights and gone back to her cash, the stock man's fifteen minutes are up, and he's pushing one of the carts down the aisle, full of boxes of spinach. Martina wonders what she missed while Sandra was going on about Josh's fight with his girlfriend. Especially, she wonders what he did when he got to the eggplant.

It's not long after nine when Sandra comes over.

"You coming?"

"I'm closing tonight," Martina says, although she isn't. "You go ahead."

"Okay then. Maybe drinks this weekend?" Sandra says over her shoulder as she pushes open the door and a whoosh of wind blows in, smelling of cigarettes and cold. Two of the stock boys are waiting for her. She sidles up between them. One puts his hand on her butt, and she playfully swats at him. Martina thinks of Dorothy, watching Blanche and her shoulder pads sail out the door night after night before getting back to another game of rummy with her mother.

Martina turns away from the window. The cashiers are all gone. There's a light on in the office. Murray's the manager on duty, and he's pretty good. Stays in the office doing whatever managers do until everybody else has left. Murray always closes up himself instead of pawning it off on the staff like some of the other managers.

Martina checks each conveyor belt, the floor, and wayward carts, scooping up abandoned receipts. There are a lot tonight. It's one of those days when nobody needs to remember what they bought. She takes a hair elastic from her wrist and bundles the receipts like a gangster's roll of cash.

"What are you doing?"

Martina's heart thunks and drops down into her stomach. Murray? She turns around. The stock man is looking at her and the roll of receipts in her hand. He doesn't look angry or like he thinks she's weird. He is smiling.

"What?"

"What are you doing with those receipts?" he asks again, gently.

"Uhh ..." Martina can't think fast enough to come up with anything other than the truth.

"I collect them," she says, shrugging.

She waits for him to frown or roll his eyes or walk away, but he does none of those things. In this fluorescent light, his hair is more blue than black. His eyes are on hers. Slowly her heart climbs back up to where it belongs.

"I have a collection too."

"Oh?"

Martina hopes he is not talking about a jar of human ears he keeps on a shelf.

"From here too."

Locks of hair from stock boys?

"Didn't you just start today?"

"Yesterday, but I was at another store before this one. I asked to be transferred over here," he clarifies.

"Why?"

"Needed something different, I guess."

"But not different enough to not work at a grocery store." Immediately Martina regrets saying this; she meant it to sound light and airy, but it came out more like baking chocolate, bitter and dusty tasting. How does Sandra look so relaxed all the time? But the stock man laughs.

"What's your collection?" Martina asks.

He pulls something out of the pocket of his fleece and shows her. It is a dented apple.

"Bruised produce."

He rubs it on the chest of his fleece, under his nametag. Doug.

"Not just bruised, of course, but any kind of damage, really."

He puts the apple back in his pocket. From his other pocket, he produces a half-squashed tangerine. Then he reaches around into his back pocket and pulls out a few fronds of dill.

"This was just left behind, not enough to sell. That's all I take, the stuff that would go into the garbage anyway."

Martina looks down at the dill in his hand and the roll of receipts in hers.

"Me too," she says. "What do you do with it?"

"I dehydrate everything in a special machine and save it for later."

This seems weird. She is trying to figure out what to say when he starts laughing.

"No, no, I'm kidding. I just think it's kind of an interesting challenge to make food out of what other people would throw away. So when I get home, I just try to make something with whatever I've got and see what it tastes like. Sometimes it's not delicious—you have to be careful to make sure all of the mould is cut off because otherwise it tastes like it's rotting inside you."

This sounds kind of terrifying. Doug is watching her carefully, which is also scary but in a different way. His Blanche eyes are the blue of dish detergent.

"But most of the time it tastes pretty good. Like with this stuff today, I'll probably do a salad with the fruit added to some lettuce I have at home from yesterday's shift. And if you put the dill with some mayonnaise—I actually bought that, you don't want to mess around with old mayo; I learned that the hard way—and some chopped up bits of other things I've got lying around, you have a nice dressing there."

This salad does not sound very tasty, but Doug is so passionate when he talks about old food that Martina is fascinated. He's put the dill and the tangerine back in his pockets, and he seems to be standing a little closer to her than he was before. His hair gleams like a blackberry.

"If you want, I can bring you a bit tomorrow?"

"Sure, I'd love that," Martina says and means it.

When she gets home, she gets everything set up at the desk. She pulls the rubber band off the bundle of receipts and smooths each one into her notebook. She leans over the book and whispers the items to herself. She is almost through the stack, almost there when she sees it, bold print, undeniable: *BBY EGGPLNT*. She freezes. In the other room: *Thank you for being a friend …* Her mother's put the DVD in again.

"Did you bring any tangerines home?" she calls out to

Martina, over the theme song.

Martina remembers the bruised tangerine that the stock man took out of his pocket and wonders how his salad is coming along.

"I'll do it tomorrow," Martina yells back, drawing a thick black line through *BBY EGGPLNT*. Making it disappear.

The Business

WHEN DARA FIRST STARTED, SHE WORKED ALONE IN HER basement, surrounded by fruit a day away from taking a turn for the worse. She forced herself not to eat any of the rectangles of milk chocolate she'd found on sale because it would have gouged her profit margin. The phone never rang, and when it did, she could hardly ever hear it over the crinkling of cellophane.

These days, though, business is good. She has a little storefront in a decent neighbourhood, and she's hired a kid to answer the phone so she can concentrate on putting the baskets together. She buys good-quality dark chocolate wholesale and nibbles on it as she works. Nowadays the fruit in her baskets wouldn't dare be overripe.

Her friends say it must be the increased demand. They tell her she's got business savvy now. But Dara knows what's behind her success: she's recommitted herself to the work. All it took was Cam leaving her and taking up with somebody else, some other teacher at his school. That was what she needed to renew her passion for the business of divorce gift baskets.

The Colours of Birds

THE SMELL OF BLACKENING EGGS WAKES MAUD LEWIS UP. SHE
opens her eyes to a squint and makes out the shape of Everett,
bent over and rattling at the woodstove.

"You're burning the eggs," she says.

"None for you, then," he says brightly.

She closes her eyes again and tries to remember the bits of
her dream that wafted away when the eggs woke her. Her dreams
are always complicated—plot twists and slips unlike the neat
threads of her waking life—but these days, there is also music in
the background, church songs from her childhood. Her sleep is
thick with it. But the dream began to disintegrate as soon as Maud
opened an eye—and a few minutes later, she can only find the
ashes of it.

The dream gone, Maud turns her attention to becoming awake.
Under the quilt, she taps the fingers of each hand against her
thigh. Her right fingers feel as though she'd knotted them into a
fist as she fell asleep, clenched until morning. She tries to move
her wrist in the beginnings of a circle, but she frowns in pain.
Stops.

Knowing her routine of checking her bones, Everett asks,
moving the pan from the stove, "And today?"

"Right one's bad," she says.

"I'm sorry, Maud," Everett says, as she knows he is.

"No eggs for me, please," Maud tells Everett gently, because she
hates the smell of burned eggs. She watches him put the two ends

of a loaf on the broiler for her instead, and in the smell of bread browning, she discovers a little more of her love for him.

1970.
Everett is kneeling in the graveyard, working in the last of the light. The mosquitoes are at him this evening, landing in the sweat of his neck and on his forehead, even his temples. Sometimes he pauses to swat at them, but mostly he keeps to his task, chipping the letters into the base of the stone: *U D*. He focuses all of himself on this task, concentrating on each press and tap, holding the letters carefully in his mouth so he doesn't make a mistake. No one is in the graveyard but Everett. Between words, he rests. He tells himself to remember to take the shrivelled, weeks-ago flowers with him when he goes—some greens and snapdragons and another wildflower he's forgotten the name of. I'll ask Maud, he thinks. Then he remembers. Grits his grief between his teeth and begins to tap out the second word: *D O*.

Everett's knees are damp and starting to ache, but he doesn't hurry. A mosquito buzzes near his ear. He leans closer to the stone and squints to see in the deepening dusk.

W L.

He rubs his eyes with the heel of his hand and colours pop behind them: red, green, blue—he thinks of the blue jays on the kettle, the backdrop of sky behind the daybed. When he opens his eyes, the blue is gone.

He leans in, peers at the stone. A mosquito hovers in front of the *L* as if it is reading, and Everett almost laughs. I must tell Maud, he thinks.

E Y.

The graveyard empties of light.

Maud is not self-conscious about having been born with almost no chin, doesn't flutter her hands in front of it or keep her eyes fixed on far-away spots like some women do, like he has done. When she looks at him, she sees him, and at first he is uncomfortable. He knows he is skinny and quiet and alone in most things. If he had a chin like hers, his hands would always be covering it. But Maud is not interested in hiding herself. At first, he is uncomfortable. Later, this shifts.

She is quiet like him, most of the time. When she paints, she hums. Soft, unrecognizable things. At the beginning, he interrupts to ask what the tune is, but she never knows. She paints and the music slips out of her mouth, unnoticed. After he stops her and she returns to her painting, there is always a silence before the humming begins again. The silence jars him, reminds him of how the little house was before Maud. The interruptions cease. He prefers knowing the sound to knowing its details.

When visitors gawk at the little house and it fills up quickly with their questions, Maud tries to explain.

"I just ... have to," is all she manages as they peer at her painted things. Stove, cups, cookie sheet, tobacco tin.

"Look! Even the egg cups!" somebody squeals.

"Look at the birds on that tin!"

"There's a meadow on this baking sheet!"

Sometimes she feels like the roof has been pulled off the house and they are being peered at and picked over by giants. Clumsy fingers grazing over the art, flicking at the curtains, knocking about the kitchen without cooking anything.

Sometimes this makes her tired, and she circles her wrists to wake herself up, arthritis opening her eyes again. She is puzzled by the interest of the visitors.

"I don't understand it, really," she says to Everett one night, just after he has blown out the candle beside the bed. Smoke floats and fades. The room smells like church.

"What, Maud?" he says.

"Why they all seem so interested. They're just my paintings. They're just what my life is, nothing more. Am I supposed to be more interested in what their lives are?"

This is much more than she usually says. There is no resentment in her. Only confusion. Everett is thinking about how to answer, when—"Oh, don't mind me," she finishes. And their old joke: "There isn't much to mind," and she turns toward him.

The rustle of the blankets as Maud moves toward him is the other sound that Everett loves.

1968.

These mornings, her routine is different. Pain covers everything; she feels it before she wakes up. These mornings, she pinches her eyes shut for the treat of opening them to the paintings. Opens them wide and waits as long as she can before blinking. She feels the muscles above her eyes pulling, a tug at the hairline, eyes wider, wider until her head aches. She looks at each painting for long moments, so long the colours melt as her eyes water.

A pair of deer standing together, looking through an opening in the trees. Maud loves the stillness of these deer, poised between her gaze and motion, between herself and the river. She paints them again from another angle and again on different surfaces. Some mornings they are especially familiar, and Maud catches them in the dregs of her dreams.

Around her bed are other pairs. Clydesdales trudging through snow (fresh snow—she loves the clean white and repaints the snow at their hooves and backs when it fades). Cattle standing in flowers, and above them, a handful of butterflies frozen in flight.

At last, Maud blinks. When she opens her eyes, they are still there, nearly the same—only a bit brighter.

Rain splatters the windshield. Everett rolls up the windows of the Ford. When they drive along the roads near their home, the wheels kick up pebbles that clink and tap against the old Model T. Maud likes the sound of the stones, but Everett winces, imagined dents plaguing him.

Outside the McGillivary house, before they get out of the car, Everett and Maud argue.

"Maud, it isn't enough."

"It's enough," she says.

"It isn't! We're not even paying for half the fuel we need to get home with what you would sell these for," he mutters, looking at the packet of newly painted cards in his hands.

Together they've made a small business out of Maud's painting. She paints, he drives, she waits while he carries the cards onto porches, knocks with one free hand. These parts of the business are clear. About money, they disagree.

Outside the McGillivarys', the close car air is too heavy to sit in. Everett clenches his jaw. "Maud," he says between his teeth.

"It's enough. I don't paint for money," she says, folding her arms under her breasts. He bites down on the something sharp he wants to say. He opens the door of the Ford, and the rain gets louder, splashes across the steering wheel. He slides the hand holding her cards inside his jacket to protect them from getting wet.

Squatting in the McGillivary foyer, Everett spreads out the cards on a dry patch of floor. Mrs. McGillivary loves the cards and buys five. Everett asks for his price and gets it. He declines a cup of tea. On the porch, he puts the few dollars difference in his shirt pocket. Glances at Maud in the passenger seat as he does it, but Maud doesn't see him. She is looking out the window at a crow perched on the fencepost despite the rain, its feathers shiny like wet tires. The crow flaps into flight as he approaches. Maud turns and notices him, and he sees in her look that the argument is over.

Everett hurries toward the Ford to get out of the rain. His shirt is beginning to cling to him.

1964.

"I'm running out of paint, again," Maud tells Everett after breakfast. She shows him what she has left: enough red for a coat or two, maybe a sled, and only a small sky's worth of blue.

She paints every day, from early morning until supper, pausing for toast and tea and a nap if she's feeling sore. Some evenings, she paints until the light goes. If sleep is slow to come, she paints by candlelight, although it is difficult to see the colours as they really are. Sometimes, when she wakes up the next morning, she is surprised by how the paintings have turned out. They are always a little disappointing in daylight. At night, there is the possibility of something hidden outside the puddle of candlelight. More to the painting than she can see.

Everett turns from the tub where he is collecting the breakfast dishes, which are nearly ready to be taken out to the pump.

"I saw that. I'll go over today. The Finches just finished another boat down at the water, and they said we could have the leftovers."

"What colour?" Maud asks.

"Blue, and they've got some leftover green and red. Maybe white? A bit of yellow from the Wilson boat, also."

"That's good. Thank you," Maud says and touches his arm with her small hand.

Everett smiles and turns back to the tub.

Later, Everett is carrying the paint back from the dock. He has left the Ford at home. It isn't a far walk from the little house.

He is carefully carrying the paint in two egg cartons, one in each hand. There is paint in each of the spaces once lived in by eggs. Blue, green, red, yellow. The inner parts of Everett's forearms are starting to ache. The cartons aren't at all heavy, but holding them like this is awkward. Everett begins to feel irritated.

Out of the corner of his eye: a flash of black.

He turns to see a crow, very close to the road, just a few steps away from a blue jay. The blue jay and crow are staring at each other. The crow is still, but the blue jay hops from foot to foot.

Watching the birds, Everett does not see the fist-sized stone in front of him. He stumbles. He nearly falls but manages to find his balance before his knees meet the road. Everett swears as he feels wet on his hands. He looks down. Paint is spilling down his hands, onto his wrists. He looks into the cartons and sees that the paint pools have become a mess of swirls, all leaking into one another. There is blue in the red cup, and yellow has slid all over the carton. The colours are ruined.

Stupid birds, Everett thinks. When he looks back, they are gone.

Back at the little house, Everett hands the soggy cartons to Maud.

"It's okay," she tells him. "I know how to use this."

Outside, she dumps all of the remaining paint into an old bucket and stirs the mixture with a wooden spoon.

That night, she dips her brush into the bucket and paints a pair of deer, their backs to her.

In the candlelight, the shade of brown is perfect.

1969.

The sound is a hum, nearly a moan. Maud's eyes and lips are both pinched tight, but the sound makes it out anyway. Everett, sitting in a wooden chair by the stove, watches her. He waits to see what the sound will turn into. But the note doesn't change. In her sleep, Maud pauses for breath and then the sound begins again, the same, steady, and grows haunting.

In the morning, Everett asks about it.

"What were you dreaming last night, Maud?"

"What?" Maud asks. "Oh. I don't quite know."

Everett shrugs and turns away. He doesn't mention the humming.

But Maud does know.

It had been a while since she thought about the baby, and longer since she dreamed of her. In the dream, she was fourteen again and in her brother's house, still Maud Dowley. And in labour, almost as it had happened, except Everett was now—impossibly—there. He was burying something under the bed as she screamed and pushed in pain. She peered over the bed and could only see his legs—bare for some reason and thin as ever—and two wooden shoes, sky blue with crows painted on them.

She woke up before the baby was born.

But the dream did not dissolve quickly as dreams usually do. All day she thinks about Everett's strange wooden dream-shoes, and wonders what he was burying under the bed.

Everett is almost home when he realizes he has left the old flowers from his parents' grave by the stones. He stops on the road and thinks for a moment about going back, but he has spent too much time there today, fixing the stone. He will get them next time, he thinks.

His knees and fingers are sore from his work in the graveyard.

He wriggles his fingers and taps them against his thighs as he walks, testing them out.

It is dark now, and Everett knows that if he bothers to look up, he will see stars. But Everett does not look up.

At home, he creaks open the painted door in the darkness. He moves slowly around the edge of the room. At the table, he fumbles for the candle and his matches.

In the limited light, he lifts his eyes and sees the pair of deer. Brown backs and legs leaning together, connected, looking away from him at something he can't see.

This Life

AFTER YOU LEFT, I HAD TO TAKE THE STREETCAR SOMEPLACE. I don't remember where, but it was rush hour. There was a skinny guy standing near me. We were both penned in by the crowd. The guy was talking out loud to himself or me or somebody else. And he said: "My brain is too sophisticated for this world. So now I'm stuck in this fucking stupid life." I inched away from him and down the streetcar steps, wishing I had the guts to tell him I understood.

The End of Everything Fun

AFTER TAI CHI, DORINDA WALKED OUT TO THE PARKING LOT WITH Alfred again. Alfred was shorter than she was, but he was in good shape for their age. The weight around his middle was more of a steering wheel than a spare tire. His blue eyes were only a little watery, and he had some hair left, thin but combed neatly. Also, his shoes had laces—they weren't slip-ons or, God forbid, Velcro. Dorinda's friend Siobhan had a husband who wore Velcro runners. There was no dignity in those shoes. When Dorinda saw Neil with those shoes on, she felt like she'd walked in on him on the toilet. No wonder Siobhan made him sleep in the basement.

It was the second time that Dorinda and Alfred had left tai chi together. The week before, Alfred had walked her to her car, chatting about how he was going to be taking care of his grandson on the weekend and smiling warmly at her as he headed to his sedan. As the week passed and it got closer to tai chi night, Dorinda found herself thinking about Alfred and hoping they'd get a chance to talk after class again. They did, and this time Alfred seemed to want to know about her, which was even nicer. He asked her if she had any grandkids and listened with interest as she explained that her daughter had decided she didn't want kids, not that Miriam had a husband to make the decision with anyway. Dorinda rolled her eyes and then felt a flutter of regret. Not only would Alfred think her awful, but as ridiculous as Miriam could be, Dorinda usually didn't criticize her to anybody but Siobhan, and only then after they'd had a few glasses of merlot and Neil had shuffled off into another room.

But Alfred didn't seem put off. In fact, he seemed to be listening very carefully. Of course, it was possible he was hard of hearing. But either way, he was paying attention in that particular way that reminded Dorinda of beery declarations of love when she was a girl, and it had been a long time since a man had paid attention to Dorinda like that. She wasn't too surprised when he asked for her number, but she was pleased.

A lot of the women Dorinda knew (or Siobhan knew and told her about) were on their own too. Some were lifelong bachelorettes—maybe quiet lesbians or women who were just smart enough not to get clogged up with a husband. Some were divorced like Dorinda. Some of them were widows—that seemed the most distinguished and honourable way to be single at their age. Dorinda wished that Bill had died. Certainly it would have been more dignified. But he had just left her, not even for somebody else but just because he didn't feel like being married anymore. It had been years, but Dorinda still remembered his face when he told her, sweaty and pale like he was ill when he was really just a coward.

Bill left when Miriam was twenty. She had moved out the year before, and so most of the time, it was just the two of them in the house. Operating in different orbits but in the same universe, more or less. It wasn't like Dorinda was so crazy about Bill, either, but when you got married, you stayed that way. He had a vaguely off-putting smell clinging to him, even when he was just out of the shower, a whiff of sweat with a barely detectable note of urine. He had grown square-shaped over the years, and he rarely said anything interesting. Still, Dorinda was angry and hurt when he left. She had planned to live out their twilight years with this sweaty square of a husband and make do about it, and then he took the option away from her.

Despite what Siobhan seemed to think, Dorinda didn't go to tai chi to meet men. She liked the slow movements. She liked how they repeated the same postures together in sequence, and if she didn't pick it up the first or tenth time, it was fine because they were just going to be doing the same moves again the next week and the week after that. She liked the feel of her weight shifting from foot to foot.

Besides, there weren't a lot of men in there to be met. There were a handful of other students, but they were all women except for Alfred and a guy named Stan who seemed to skip more classes than he attended. The tai chi instructor was a man, but he was young, sort of, although it was kind of hard to tell. He could be fifty, or he could be eighty. In the first class, he told them all about how good tai chi was for your body, that it could be as good for you as swimming. Maybe the instructor was like a vampire, getting older like everybody else but keeping the body and face of his fifty-or-eighty-year-old self.

Alfred called the day after he asked for her number. This was another thing about Alfred to like—he didn't dither around and keep a person waiting.

"Is Dorinda there, please?"

Dorinda mentally snorted. Did he think she lived in a colony of other women? Although she supposed some women her age lived with their children. Maybe Alfred thought it was Miriam answering the phone. God help me, Dorinda thought. If Miriam moved in, it would be the end of eating those crunchy Cheezies in bed, the end of boozy coffees on Sunday mornings, the end of wearing her muumuus without reproach. The end of everything fun and the beginning of house arrest.

"This is she," Dorinda said primly. She was out of practice being ladylike.

"This is Alfred. From tai chi?" As opposed to the dozens of other men who might be calling her. But Dorinda was glad he didn't presume he was the only man in her life. Which, of course, he was, unless you counted Velcro Neil, which Dorinda didn't.

"Yes, Alfred. How are you?"

They exchanged pleasantries, and then there was a pause.

"So ... would you like to go out with me this Sunday evening?"

Hmmm. Not as solid an offer as a Friday or Saturday night, but who was she to be so choosy? Maybe he had something special planned. Or who knows—maybe Sunday was date night, now. It had been a while.

"Sure."

After that, Alfred offered to pick her up at six thirty. She gave him her address, then gave it to him again after he'd put the phone down to find a pen. When they got off the phone, she started thinking about what she might wear, and she felt a strange feeling in her stomach, like there were waves in there or something. It had been so long since Dorinda had felt nervous about anything that it took her all afternoon to figure out what the feeling was. What am I nervous for? Stupid old woman, she thought to herself as she flipped through the clothes in her closet, looking for something decent.

"Let's go shopping!" Siobhan shouted.

"You don't need to yell. I'm not deaf yet."

"Sorry, I'm so used to Neil," Siobhan said at a volume that was only slightly lower.

"I'm sure I can just wear something I have. Or borrow something from you." This last thing was a charitable gesture on Dorinda's part, since anything Siobhan had would be like a tent on her.

"No, let's go shopping. I'll pick you up later this afternoon, and we'll go to the mall."

Siobhan loved driving. Dorinda didn't like to drive unless it was an emergency, and only if it was an emergency in daylight, and only when it wasn't raining or too sunny. Siobhan also loved shopping. At her house, when Dorinda went to put empty wine bottles in the recycling container, there was always a lot of packaging and boxes from Siobhan's latest online shopping binge. It was amazing Siobhan had anything to live on with the way she spent. Probably Neil had always been a good saver, though. He had that look about him.

At the mall, everything was too flowery.

"It's because it's spring," Siobhan said. "Don't be so sour."

"I'm not sour. I just want a solid colour."

"Fine. But no muumuus."

As if she would wear a muumuu on a date. Dorinda rolled her eyes.

"Ooh, look at this!" Siobhan tugged something off a rack and held it up to herself. It was a puffy, flowery smock that Dorinda wouldn't be caught dead in.

"For me?"

"No, for me!"

"Aren't we shopping for me?"

"Fine. You're such a stick in the mud sometimes."

Dorinda wandered deeper into the store. On the sale rack, there was a lovely white eyelet dress that reminded Dorinda of things she used to wear to the beach when she was much younger, just see-through enough that the boys could spot the outline of her bikini underneath.

She sighed and picked up some sensible grey slacks to try.

"Oh, God. Live a little!" Siobhan said when she saw what Dorinda had in her hand.

"I like these." Dorinda frowned. She should have taken a taxi to the mall and come by herself.

"Well, at least try them with a bit of colour." Siobhan held out a turquoise top with a scoop neck. It looked like it would fit Dorinda perfectly.

"That's not too bad, actually." Now it was Siobhan who rolled her eyes.

When Dorinda came out of the change room, Siobhan tried to whistle. It sounded more like a child blowing out birthday candles, but Dorinda got what she meant. She had to agree. The pants fit her nicely and showed off her figure, still fairly trim really, despite the Cheezies and age, thanks to her walking and tai chi and small meals. And the turquoise top was flowy and flattering. Siobhan was definitely a good shopper.

"Alfred is going to die when he sees you," Siobhan said as

they stood at the cash.

"I certainly hope not," Dorinda said, suddenly picturing Siobhan showing up at Alfred's funeral to comfort her, Neil trailing behind her in a black suit and Velcro shoes.

On Sunday, Dorinda started getting ready for the date around three, just to be safe. By five, the tops of her new slacks were wrinkled from sitting. The top covered some of the wrinkles. Dorinda thought about changing into different pants, but she didn't want to look too pressed and uptight, so she kept the wrinkles in the slacks. In the bathroom, she stared into the medicine cabinet mirror, wishing she had a smoother face to change into. Inside she felt as young as the girl with the eyelet dress over her bikini, walking with purpose across the sand, knowing the boys were watching her legs, her swivelling hips. Until the next time she saw her reflection and the girl in the eyelet dress poofed away and the sand blew back into Dorinda's eyes, stinging and making it hard to see anything at all.

By the time Alfred arrived at quarter past six, Dorinda had put two thousand steps on her pedometer just from pacing around the apartment. He was wearing khakis and a burgundy golf shirt, his hair neat as usual, and he smiled broadly—a bit nervously, she thought—as he stepped into her foyer.

"You look lovely," he said.

She suggested he come in for a glass of wine, but he said they should probably get going.

"Where are we going?"

"Oh, you'll see. It's not far from here. Do you mind walking?"

Bill never wanted to walk anywhere, but she had always preferred it to driving.

"Not at all. Just let me get a sweater."

She went upstairs to her bedroom to get it, leaving him in the hallway. When she came back downstairs, he was jingling the change in his pocket just like Bill used to do. She shivered and pulled the door behind them and locked it.

"So, I wanted to take you somewhere special, somewhere that

was really me," Alfred said as they walked.

Dorinda wondered again where they were going. Maybe a particular park or a pub where everybody would smile and pat Alfred's back when they walked in.

"That's nice," she said and regretted it. Alfred was going to think she was bland. "What's your grandson been up to this week?"

He grinned and talked animatedly about the little boy as they turned down a side street and then onto another. At a church she'd walked by many times but never gone in, he took her elbow. Dorinda was beginning to feel uneasy. A slim man passed them on the sidewalk and nodded at Alfred. He nodded back. The man went ahead of them, pulling open the door to the church basement.

Inside, everybody seemed to know Alfred, and some of them even patted him on the back. But there was nothing to drink except coffee in Styrofoam cups. Dorinda was getting a feeling about where they might be, and this was no pub.

"Welcome, everyone," said a woman at the front of the room. "Let's get started. My name is Andrea, and I'm an alcoholic."

Siobhan swallowed another gulp of merlot. Her lips were looking bloodier with every glass.

"I mean, it's kind of nice in a way, right? He wanted to be honest with you, right from the start."

"I guess, but a proper date would have been nice."

"He's obviously into wellness, right? The tai chi and the AA ..."

Dorinda refilled her glass and wondered what Alfred would say if he knew about the Cheezies and the merlot and the muumuus. Suddenly it seemed like an awful lot of effort, the whole process of revealing yourself to someone else, one ugly bit at a time.

Neil came into the room.

"Goodnight, ladies," he said, doing a weird little bow and shuffling back out of the room before they could say anything.

Siobhan grinned at Dorinda with her big, bloody mouth and

held out her glass for a top up. Dorinda rolled her eyes and started laughing at all of it, at Neil and Alfred and Siobhan and especially herself, getting all dressed up and nervous and pacing around the apartment in her wrinkly new slacks and old face.

The White Stain

LEE KRASNER LOVED PARTIES BEFORE SHE MET JACKSON POLLOCK. She loved the excitement she felt when standing on the doorstep after ringing the bell. Poised on the edge of the evening before the host opened the door and swept her inside in a flurry of kisses and coats.

Pretty girls weren't as good at parties as she was. Sure, they were lovely to look at, but you could only stare at a lily for so long, Lee felt, before its tips seemed to wilt and brown under the scrutiny. When Lee moved through a room, winking and squeezing shoulders and poking her sharp jokes into places they didn't belong, she felt better than pretty. She felt significant.

After she met Jackson, it wasn't as much fun anymore. She still chatted and enjoyed herself, some nights, but there was always the risk of an Incident, so she could never really relax. He might fall or scream or piss or, at the very least, spill something too bright on something too expensive. So she was never quite listening, and people noticed. It is hard to make small talk with someone whose ears are tuned to shattering glass.

Tonight is the first party after Jackson's death. Lee hasn't been farther than the garden in weeks or longer, it's hard to remember. She has declined party invitations for months. She doesn't want to go tonight, either, but she was too tired to say no this time; it was too much trouble to muster up the negative. Over the phone, her silence was taken as acquiescence.

After bathing, she stands in front of the wardrobe, completely still. Fat drops splash down her back and onto the hardwood. She looks at her clothes. Azure, vermilion, raspberry. Magenta, green, cadmium yellow. Her eyes hurt. She rests them on an ivory blouse and listens to her breath for a moment before facing the task of dressing. But the decision is too difficult. Lee feels a stir of panic. She stares at the colours in the closet, and eventually her eyes grow used to them again. She begins naming them to keep herself calm. Aubergine, carrot, alizarin crimson. She names the colours of every button and shoelace. She takes apart paisleys and flowered patterns, breaks them down into each thread of discrete colour. Rose. Cobalt. Then she names the colours that make up the closet itself. Cerulean doors with a lavender interior. There are stockings crumpled on the floor of the closet—midnight blue—and she squints to name the lint on the square of carpet under her shoes. Malachite and sepia. Lee peers into the closet, looks along the shelves and in the dark corners at the back, but there are no colours left unnamed.

Wrapped in a towel, she backs away and sinks down onto the bed, listing to the side like a ship, the towel coming untucked. It is too much effort to tuck it back in, so she lies on the bed and waits for something to happen. The pillow grows damp from her hair and face, and the towel is wet on top of the crumpled sheet. It will be a little more comfortable if Lee rolls over. She starts to shiver and doesn't move.

The phone is ringing. Lee lies still. It rings and rings. She drags herself off the bed, leaving the towel behind, shaking her head to get rid of the haze of sleep.

"Hello?"

"Lee, you haven't left yet?" Anna sounds annoyed. It's very noisy in the background. Lee's shoulders inch up tensely. Someone is laughing too loudly, a shrill noise that covers the other sounds of the party: clinking, low music, a dozen conversations, a "Fuck!" after a smash, and the scurrying around to clean something up. That's what Lee hears as she tries to figure out what to say.

"Lee?"

"I'm here."

"I know. That's the problem. Why aren't you here? People are asking."

"I got held up. I'm coming." Lee rubs her face with the hand not holding the receiver. She can't figure out how to get out of this. They're expecting her. She sighs.

"You promise?"

"Yes. I'm coming. Goodbye."

Lee is irritated. She realizes she can't remember what the party is for, if there's some kind of celebration she's forgotten to mark. It takes too much energy to both remember this and attempt dressing, so Lee goes back to the closet. She stands in front of it, closes her eyes and reaches in, swims her hand around in the dark air and stops at the back of the closet. As soon as she feels cloth, she tugs down and pulls it toward her. The freed hanger clatters against another. The wood sounds soft and hollow. Lee opens her eyes. She is holding a flowing white dress with capped sleeves. It doesn't hurt her eyes. She peers at it. The white is bone.

Lee backs out of the closet and steps into the dress. She pulls on the crumpled midnight-blue stockings and slips on the shoes nearest to her, some old ochre shoes she gardens in sometimes. In the kitchen, she picks up the keys to the truck and hears the clink and slide of the keys coming off the Formica into her hand. When she looks down, she sees a smudge of white on her wrist. She stares at it. Zinc white. She tries to think of when it is from, but she can't remember. She's been painting at night in shades of white, finding colours too sharp, too noisy. But the last few days, she's been in bed and hasn't been interested in finding her way to canvas. The white stain must have been there for several days. She realizes that her hands must be very dirty and holds them to her face to smell them. Her hands smell like dried grass and copper. She goes back into the bedroom and takes a bracelet from the bureau, a green cuff that covers the stain. The phone starts to ring again. Lee walks quickly to the door and lets the screen slam after her as she ducks into the pickup, turns on the engine, looks behind her to reverse and pull away.

It is too cold to be wearing the white dress, Lee realizes by the time she arrives at the party. Although it is only October, the air is turning. When she closes the door to the truck, she hears the creak of cold trees. As she draws closer to the house, the noises of the party leak out and spread toward her, a mess of laughter and voices.

"Lee! Finally. Come in, come in!" Lee feels her chest shrink under her skin. She follows the hostess into the foyer.

"Anna, shut the door! It's freezing!" someone shouts.

"Sorry I'm late."

"Oh, it's fine. Better late than never!" Anna trills.

Lee winces. She can't remember what she used to bring to parties—wine probably, didn't help Jackson, why do that? She says nothing and follows Anna into a loud room full of party guests. Lee's shoulders tighten. She sees a corner with an unoccupied chair and begins to weave her way through the crowd. As she passes, people grab her elbow, give her sympathetic looks. Someone touches her back. The faces are red and sweaty, some of them; others are thin and sallow. She keeps her eyes on the chair.

"So sorry, Lee. He was a great painter," someone says to her left. She nods in the direction of the voice but doesn't stop. She reaches the chair and sinks into it, feeling like she's been on a hike instead of just crossing a room. She thinks about the relief of going back into her house, creeping back into bed. Someone hands her a drink, and she clutches the tumbler tightly without tasting what's in it. What these people don't know is that she feels a thud of pressure in her chest, and her thoughts start repeating themselves: get out, get out, get out of this. Sometimes, being in the presence of other people's voices is physically painful. It is suddenly too loud. Shut up, shut up, shut up. She remembers that she used to not feel this way. She remembers spending hours on the phone making arrangements for Jackson, bargaining with art dealers, trying to get him shows. She doesn't remember feeling a thud of pressure in her chest when people spoke to her then. Now she sits and looks at the blur around her, and she notices herself tightening and tightening. The clash of the party presses against her, closer and closer, and it's so noisy she imagines screaming would not attract any attention.

"I can't do this. This is too social. I have to go," she says and stands up, putting the still-full tumbler on a piano bench nearby. The cluster of guests nearest to her stop talking and look at her strangely. Two of them glance at her but look away quickly, perhaps afraid her next words will be for them directly. The third man in the group says, "Oh," and moves out of the way for her to pass. Lee feels a flash of gratitude before the fear comes back. As she pushes again through the crowd, she sees a clock mounted above the doorway, its face soothing white. Like a dancer, she sticks her gaze to this spot, to the clock, to keep herself from falling. She squints to see where the hands are. Halfway across the room, she can read the time. It's been less than twenty minutes since she followed Anna into the party. Lee is stunned—it feels like hours she's been trapped in the corner. She thinks of butterflies on pins and wonders if it is the pinning that kills them, an excruciating slow death on display. Lee shivers and shoves.

"Hey, watch it!"

"That's Lee—leave her—"

The phrases float around her. As she walks past a pair of squat men with scaly skin, she hears one of them muttering: "That face? ... Pollock ... but she does have a good body."

But she does have a good body. This is not the first time Lee has overheard this sort of appraisal, and knows it has happened in many conversations she has not heard. The worst is when she is meant to hear it, when Jackson said it in a small room, as if to remind her of her good fortune. How lucky she was to be the one who would go home with him to watch him crash into bedroom furniture and fall asleep half-undressed, his breath rancid and jagged on her neck. She turns back to look at the men. One is fatter than the other and redder in his hairless face. His head, too, is almost entirely bald, and the empty ground of his scalp is flaking away in white bits, as if trying to follow the hair. She decides he is the one who has spoken. She moves up close to him, closer, until she must be breathing on him. He looks startled, his blue eyes blinking. She takes his drink out of his hands and is still for a moment. She imagines pouring it down his head, his blue eyes and flaky skin drowning in brown liquor. Instead, she dumps the drink on the rug at his feet. He looks confused. They both look down and see the brown liquid quickly seeping into the carpet in an ugly, undrinkable stain. Lee turns and walks out of the party, down the hall, and into the crisp, easier air.

At home, Lee moves to the window and opens it wider. At her worst, the one thing she can bear, the only thing that isn't searing, is the sound of wind. Outside, the trees are slowly undressing themselves for winter. Many of their leaves are already covering the wild garden, and more fall as the wind takes them. She wonders why trees are naked during the coldest months, when everything else does its shedding in summer. She shivers in her thin white dress and lies down on her bed. She curls further into herself instead of shutting the window, sticks her feet under a knitted blanket piled at the foot of the bed. The wind cycles from crescendo to silence, and it seems to her that it grows louder each time it rises. This soothes her, and she slides into half sleep, listening to the wind.

A few hours later, Lee is awake again. The moon peeks in at her. The wind has stopped. Lee turns over, fidgets, rolls over again. Sleep pulls away from her, out of reach. She kicks the blanket from her feet, and it slumps to the floor as she stands up.

Outside, moonlight stains the garden. She smells the pinching air and picks out the scents she can identify: thick, dark dirt and leaves about to disintegrate, the ones hidden under the newest layer. Shaken there by the wind. She wonders how instrumental the wind is in the shifting of the seasons. Without wind, would autumn stay? She thinks of Anna, imagines her fluttering around her living room, knows if Anna hadn't called, she could have skipped the party completely. Lee sees her gathering highball glasses of melted ice cubes, emptying ashtrays, opening the window to let the cold chase out the tight, stale air. She sees her bending to pick up a scrap of napkin and gasping as she finds a stain, the colour of old blood and now the size of an hors d'oeuvre platter. Anna spits out a gob of curse words in the empty room. Lee smiles.

In the garden, it is quiet except for scritching at the corner of the overgrown vegetable patch. A fat raccoon lifts his head and stares at Lee for a minute before ambling away. She stays still and waits, hoping the animal will return and finish what he was up to in the corner. If she stands completely still, doesn't even shiver, maybe the raccoon will think she's gone and will come back to his apple core or garbage or babies. Lee tries to become invisible, still as stone, but she is alone in the dark garden. There is no one to not see her.

Thanksgiving

AALIYAH'S COUSIN USED TO BE FOUR HUNDRED POUNDS. RIGHT before Thanksgiving three years ago, he decided to go on a juice fast.

He sipped on green juice at the dinner table and passed the sweet-potato casserole to his aunt, holding it carefully at the edges because the dish was hot, trying not to smell it.

Aaliyah's cousin served pieces of ham to his little nephew with tongs and topped it with a ring of pineapple. He finished his green juice after that and started on a carrot one.

He scooped whipped cream onto a piece of pecan pie before passing it to his grandmother. The carrot juice was just as delicious.

The next year, Aaliyah's cousin was only a hundred and fifty pounds. His aunts and uncles and cousins and nieces and nephews told him how wonderful he looked. His grandmother frowned and watched him nibble on salad and pass the sweet potato and ham without taking anything except a quarter of a pineapple ring.

"Go to the doctor. And eat some pie," she said to Aaliyah's cousin in the kitchen afterwards.

To make his grandmother happy, Aaliyah's cousin went to the doctor (but he wouldn't take the pie). The doctor told him to gain a bit of weight back, that he had accomplished so much, but there was such a thing as going too far.

So Aaliyah's cousin started eating. He went back to eating everything he had been when he was four hundred pounds, and by the next Thanksgiving, he had gained everything back. His grandmother found him in the kitchen, polishing off the pecan pie before the rest of the family arrived for dinner.

"This isn't good, either," she told him.

"I know," said Aaliyah's cousin, around a bite of pie.

So the next day, Aaliyah's cousin went back to the doctor, but on the way in, he stumbled on a step and felt his ankle twist and snap as he went down heavily.

In the hospital, they did some tests and X-rays, and they discovered a tumour inside him, huge and menacing, and the family brought him juice in his hospital bed and leftovers from Thanksgiving, spread out like a picnic, but nobody felt much like eating.

Clara and Rosemary

CLARA DOESN'T NOTICE THAT HENRY IS DEAD UNTIL SHE COMES back into their bedroom after her exercises and tea. For months afterwards, awake in the dark early mornings, she will go over and over it in her head. She will wonder how long the room had been too still and blame the dream for making her not see.

Maybe she had the dream because she'd eaten too late, or because Henry had been even quieter than usual. She could have asked him about it before bed, but after fifty-six years, Clara knew when to leave it alone.

It was the kind of dream that felt like it was trying to claw its way out of her sleep and into the room. That's what Clara tells her cousin Rosemary after the funeral. Rosemary nods, pats Clara's hand, and steers her toward the cucumber sandwiches.

In the dream, mice were skittering in the walls and racing along the headboard. She looked down and one was draped around her throat like a scarf. She screamed and flung it away, but another ran over her bare ankle. Something was making her hand wet. She lifted her palm off the sheet, and there was a dissected rat, splayed open, red guts spilling onto the bed. She could see the glint of eyes and flicking grey tails everywhere she looked in their room. That was the worst part, she thinks, lying in bed in the dark early mornings. In the dream, she was in their bedroom, exactly as it was, Henry asleep beside her as she shook off mice and wiped away rat gut. Everything was the same except it was suddenly awful.

Rosemary and her son Michael drive Clara back to the apartment after the funeral. Clara's feet ache from standing, and someone from Henry's old office squeezed her hand too hard and the joints in her fingers throb now. Rosemary sits next to her in the back seat and holds Clara's hand lightly in her small, soft palm. Michael hums as he drives through the slushy streets. It sounds like the wet asphalt is shushing them as the car pushes through leftover snow.

Rosemary is quiet. After Donald died, Rosemary told Clara how awkward people were, how almost everyone rushed to fill the air with talk instead of letting her be. At Henry's funeral, there were too many people saying too many things. When Clara saw that other people's mouths had stopped squirming out words, she made hers move, and then the people went away and more replaced them. On the way home, Clara tries to think about who had actually been there—is she supposed to send thank-you cards for this? No, probably she isn't—but the only one she can remember seeing is Rosemary.

At the apartment building, Rosemary and Michael get out with her. Michael takes her arm and carefully leads her up the sidewalk. Rosemary leans on her cane and follows them slowly. At the door, Clara rummages through her purse with stiff fingers until she finds the keys. Rosemary comes up beside her.

"I'll come back over around suppertime with a pasta bake, but are you sure you don't want me to come up with you now?"

Rosemary's grey eyes look right at hers. Clara feels safe, then afraid.

"I need a little time," Clara says. "I think I need to lie down."

"Of course. Michael will bring me back around five, then, all right?"

Clara nods and watches Michael take his mother's arm as they walk back to the car. Such a good boy he's always been, taking care of his mother after his father left. He is grown and has his own life now, but he still checks in with his mother every day. For the first time in many years, Clara feels that old tiring ache. Wishes she had a grown child to walk with her back to the car.

The apartment smells like old bacon grease from the suite

below them and overripe fruit that Henry bought and did not eat. Clara stands in the doorway in her car coat and rain hat, purse over her arm, and the grief is sand in her throat and glue under her boots and skittering mice in her head. She stands there in the doorway, not knowing what else to do, until Rosemary comes back with the pasta bake at five and gently moves past her, into the empty apartment, clinking around as she begins to make tea.

*

Clara is the first person Rosemary calls when her brother dies.

"Oh, poor Donald," Clara says. "Want me to come over?"

"Can you meet me at his apartment instead? In two hours?"

"Of course." As Clara hangs up, Rosemary can hear her calling Henry into the kitchen.

The apartment is only a few minutes' drive from Rosemary's place, but she isn't sure what she will find there. Maybe some things she won't want anyone to see. Not even Clara.

Michael is still at school. She scribbles him a note that she will be back soon and to wait for her. Part of her wants to leave a note that says, "Uncle Donald died," but Rosemary hates leaving notes that say anything important. As tough as Michael tries to be these days, she wants to be there beside him when he finds out. When Frank left, Michael couldn't even read very well yet, but he stood beside her chair as she read the note, his small hand on her shoulder. She sat there for a long time, rereading it, and he didn't move, his skin warm and making the polyester damp.

Donald's worker called the ambulance after she found him, and the paramedics called the coroner, and somewhere in there somebody called Rosemary. The worker—it was Maria on Mondays—had apparently found him on the toilet. Rosemary didn't get details, didn't want anything to supplement or verify what she could already see in her head and will keep seeing, through the funeral and for a long time after: Donald, pants around his ankles, head leaning against the wall, mouth and eyes open. Skin grey and leathery and the room filled with stink.

Clara is seven and Rosemary is eight. They are crouched down, making an elaborate little town in the dirt. Clara is building a library out of small stones and drawing books inside of it with a twig. Rosemary is making houses by scraping piles of dirt together with her fingers and adding bits of leaf for windows and doors. Her nails are dirty, and her palms are red from leaning on them. She's almost finished with the houses.

"I'm going to do a park next. Here, behind the library." Rosemary points at the spot with her stick.

Clara nods and keeps working on the library, wishing she'd thought of a park first but knowing the town won't be complete without it. Rosemary thinks of everything just a little bit faster than Clara does, and her ideas are always good. It was her idea to build the town in the first place, and they've been working on it all morning, and it's not even a little bit boring yet.

"Rosemary! Can you go find your brother and tell him it's time for lunch?" Rosemary's mother calls from the house.

Rosemary and Clara stand up and brush the dirt off their tights and skirts. They start off in search of Donald, Rosemary a few steps ahead.

Donald is at the edge of the train tracks, poking at something with a stick.

"Donald! Mum says come home for lunch!" Rosemary yells, but Donald doesn't move. She sighs. Her brother doesn't ever seem to see or hear her. She has no idea what he thinks about or cares about. It's strange to live in the next room to someone for your whole life and not know them at all.

Rosemary and Clara come up behind Donald, and then they can see what he's doing.

The rat's belly has been ripped open by something sharp. The dirt around it is bloody. From where they're standing, they can see one of the rat's eyes. Clara gasps and Rosemary reaches for her hand. Donald dips the stick into the rat's stomach and pulls out a knot of its guts, tosses it into the bushes. The rat's eye flinches.

Clara starts to cry, and Donald turns and sees them at last. His face is red and scary. Rosemary holds tight to Clara's hand. But Donald doesn't say anything, just pushes past them and heads back to the house, flinging the stick onto the tracks.

*

When Rosemary finds out she is pregnant, she calls Clara right away.

"Oh, that's wonderful," Clara says, disappointment dragging her down onto the kitchen floor. She can see her reflection in the oven door.

"I'm ... sorry," Rosemary says awkwardly.

"Don't be. You've been trying too. At least one of us is having luck!" Clara tries to laugh, but it comes out more like a cough.

"Really. I'm so happy for you," Clara says and doesn't even care if it is convincing. After they hang up, she slides down until she can't see her reflection in the oven anymore. She lies on the floor, staring at the detritus under the stove—a few kernels of corn, crumbs, something black she doesn't want to think too hard about.

On top of everything else that is awful, Rosemary's new little one won't have her Clara. For years, they have talked about having two little girls who would be best friends. It is starting to look like Clara won't be able to hold up her end of the bargain. On the linoleum, Clara cries and cries: for the little lonely one growing in Rosemary's belly, for Henry, and then, for a long time, for herself and the ache that never lets her be, not even when she is sleeping.

Eventually, she pushes herself up to start dinner. Henry will be home soon, and she doesn't want him to worry about her any more than he already does.

*

Rosemary slides the pasta bake into the oven and puts the kettle on again. She looks over at Clara, sitting by the window and staring out at the street, tea gone cold beside her. She's been here first and knows the worst part is coming. Rosemary dreamed of rat gut too, when Donald died, but she never told anyone. There's something else she's never told anyone, not even Clara.

When Donald died, she felt relieved. Lighter, and close to glad. But Rosemary has been watching Clara and Henry together for fifty-six years. She knows that Clara is not relieved. She knows she does not feel anything but awful.

The Internet People

CLAUDIA'S JOB GETS MIXED REACTIONS ON FIRST DATES. WHEN she says she is an assessor at a nuclear power plant, the men usually ask what that means, and she says: "Quality assurance. I manage permits and check that we're up to code. I'm one of the people who make sure everything's running smoothly."

"Wow, that's exciting," the men say.

Maybe sometimes they mean it. But sometimes they say it with dead eyes, checking their phones under the table or asking if she's going to finish her tzatziki.

Actually, although she understands it is not fashionable to say so, Claudia finds her work satisfying. Quality assurance work makes her feel responsible and useful. Sometimes the men ask if she is afraid of the radiation.

"Nuclear energy is really very safe these days," she says, feeling like a human brochure.

Usually the men who ask this change the subject, start talking about their work or an innocuous current event, a hospitalized celebrity or an unusual shift in the weather. Sometimes they order dessert at this point. This time, the man across the table—his name is Leon—signals for the cheque right after she's said this. Leon is clearly furious.

Leon is very different from Claudia, but she has never been one of those people who end up dating themselves. He found her online and contacted her first, and his attention made her a little more interested than she might have been otherwise. In Leon's profile, he talked about wanting to change the world in small ways and how he saw surfing as a spiritual experience. In his picture, he was browned by the sun, leaning against his surfboard and narrowing his eyes against the light. She thought he seemed healthy, at peace. When they met outside the restaurant, he looked a bit more like George Costanza than she would have liked, but she wasn't about to end the date early over it.

She watches him wave the server over.

"We're ready to leave. Can you bring the machine over, please?" Claudia pulls her wallet out of her purse.

"No, no," Leon says, jaw clenching under his skin. "It's my pleasure." His eyes are hard.

"Is everything okay, Leon?"

"I just can't understand how you can do that. Haven't you read *The Fate of the Earth*?"

"Sure," she says, although she hasn't.

"With all of the trouble that nukes have caused, how can you go into work every day and contribute to that?" His voice is getting louder.

Claudia focuses on putting her wallet back into her purse slowly and deliberately. Puts her keys in a pocket that will be easy to reach into once she gets to the door. Home.

"And not only do you swallow the shit they put in the pamphlets, but you spout it back out like it's true!"

Well, it is true, Claudia thinks, but she is a little bit afraid now and doesn't say this.

She glances at Leon. He's balding on top, but his stringy hair is long, spreading down over his collar like roots. Red splotches are showing up on his neck. His round face almost seems to be quivering. His eyes are dark chunks in his face under his eyebrows, the hairs pointing in all different directions, messed up from when he rubbed his hand across them a second ago. His breath sounds loud and ragged. Claudia is afraid he'll have a heart attack before they've left the restaurant. She decides to follow his example and forget her manners.

She stands up, takes her coat from the back of the chair, and pulls the strap of her purse up over her shoulder.

"Thank you for dinner. Don't call me," she says, as if that were still a possibility.

The following week, she has another date, a Thursday evening dinner plan. On Wednesday, Claudia has lunch with her friend June.

"Any interesting prospects?" June asks, a spot of mayonnaise in the corner of her mouth. Claudia wipes the corner of her own mouth, but June doesn't take the hint.

"A date tomorrow. A new guy," Claudia says.

Even though it is a perfectly acceptable way for people in their thirties to date these days, Claudia feels a twinge of shame when one of her paired-up friends asks how the internet dating is going. Like if she were only a little thinner or a sliver smarter or a tad funnier, she wouldn't have to keep tossing out the fishing line into the dark and hoping for the best.

Also, there's something exhausting about it: all that blooming and shrinking of hope. Usually Claudia is not a person who gets tired. She is always asleep by quarter to ten and wakes at six thirty without hitting snooze. After twenty minutes on the treadmill and a shower deliberately broken up with spurts of cold water, she is alert, and she stays alert all day.

At work, she sends emails and completes inspection reports. She works on assessments at her desk and goes to meetings with project managers about welding procedures and radiation protection. She drinks a coffee on the way in and has an Earl Grey tea around three. She doesn't yawn much unless someone else starts it first. The days, even when they feel long, are never unreasonably so. Claudia likes the rhythm of her weeks most of the time, her orderly work, her lunches with June.

"Well, he can't be any worse than the last one," June says. "He acted like you're on the Manhattan Project!"

Claudia scoops up a spoonful of tuna from the top of her salad. A caper bursts between her teeth, salty and sharp.

"I really think you should tell the internet people how

terrible he was."

"The internet people? You know that there aren't miniature humans working away inside the computers, right?"

June rolls her eyes, but she's laughing.

"I mean the people who run the website. Tell them they should attach a warning to him, or maybe an R-rating, like a horror movie."

"It's not like he hit me."

"No, he didn't hit you. But anybody that goes from zero to rage that quickly should not be allowed to meet new people, especially nice people."

Claudia feels a rush of gratefulness for June, who is dipping a french fry into a glob of ketchup and glaring at it like the crispy stick is Leon reincarnated. Claudia is touched by June's outrage and is glad they met for lunch today. Watching June eat, Claudia tries not to stare at the mayonnaise splotch still by her mouth, stubborn as the last bit of snow that clings to the ground at the end of winter.

Claudia arrives first. The bar is in her neighbourhood and not very busy, just the way she likes it. This time they are having drinks instead of dinner, which makes it easier to complete an early extraction if need be. When Claudia first started meeting men from the site, she never plotted escape plans in advance like this. Experience has stomped on her optimism with its clompy, muddy boots. Claudia sips from her pint glass. The beer is tepid.

She recognizes Dean from his profile picture. He's cute in the way she likes best, like he's just climbed down off a mountain after years of living there, seeing no one. The Anti-Claud, June would call him. His scruffy beard and hair look careless, like they're supposed to look, rather than curated. She smiles and waves him over.

But there is something wrong with him. Maybe he's high or very tired, but after each question Claudia asks, there is a silence so long it feels like a Quaker wedding she went to once.

The bar is quiet enough. He can hear her, and the questions aren't difficult.

"You said you liked camping, right? Have you ever been to Algonquin?"

Claudia doesn't really know anything about camping, but June used to go to Algonquin Park every summer with her family when she was a kid. It seems an easy way to start a conversation. But Claudia could finish an incident report in the time he takes to answer. He looks at his beer as though the answer might be floating in there like a fleck of ash or skin.

The bartender cleans glasses while she watches the television on mute. An old man walks in and heads for a stool near the TV. The bartender smiles and greets him. She calls him Doc. Claudia is still waiting for an answer. She drinks. Finally, he speaks.

"Nope," he says.

They sit in silence for a while. Claudia swirls what's left of her beer.

"How was work?" she says, and she is almost finished her beer by the time he answers.

"Oh, it was okay."

Claudia remembers a sloth she saw on vacation in Costa Rica once, moving languidly down a tree trunk. She watched him make his way down for his weekly bowel movement, grey furry handbag of a body moving like a glacier.

He speaks again.

"I might have gotten fired, actually. I'm not sure. But it's okay because I think I'm done with being an arborist. My cousin and me might go into the paper business."

Suddenly Claudia feels deeply, into-the-bones tired, and she just wants to be home and sleeping.

"Okay, thanks for the beer; I've gotta go," she says.

Dean doesn't look surprised, just nods and stares into his glass. Only a quarter of the beer is gone.

When Claudia gets home, she deletes his emails and falls asleep with the light still on.

The day after her date with Dean, Claudia hits snooze for the first time in years. Normally when her alarm goes, Claudia is already awake, or if not, glad to be awoken. Today she goes on the treadmill for ten minutes and is exhausted. She stands in the shower for a long time and doesn't turn the knob to cold once. She figures it's just been a bad sleep, maybe a nightmare she can't remember. It's Friday and maybe that has something to do with it. Maybe it's been a long week. She stands in the water, and for the first time in four years, wishes she didn't have to go to work.

After her coffee, she is more awake. She gives her assistant, Laura, a list of meetings to book. She works on a spreadsheet in preparation for a meeting with her manager. Normally her fingers fly over the keyboard like she's one of those people who type the captions for television or a court stenographer on *Law & Order*. But her fingers feel slow today. Before finishing the spreadsheet, she takes a break to buy coffee from the cafeteria. She wonders how long it would take Dean to finish a cup of coffee. She gulps too big a mouthful, but the coffee isn't hot enough to hurt.

After work, June comes over for a rehash of the date. Claudia orders a pizza with kale and bacon. She makes them mimosas.

"Is this brunch? Why are we having mimosas?"

"That's what I have. That's what you're getting." June and Claudia have been friends for seventeen years. Sometimes they are each other's cold water splash.

Claudia sips her mimosa like Dean to demonstrate.

"He wasn't seriously that slow."

Claudia counts five breaths before she answers.

"He was."

June laughs. "What is wrong with these guys?"

"What isn't?" Claudia says and feels a yawn growing inside her like a lump.

Sometimes when Claudia is running on the treadmill, she wants to stop as soon as she's started. But if she just runs a little further in place, just a few more minutes, the feeling goes away. Scrolling through dating profiles on Sunday afternoon, Claudia decides to push through until the tired feeling goes away. She reads the profile of a man who is older than she is, divorced, with eyes that look warm in his picture. Daniel is looking for someone to listen to birds and eat chips with. That does it. She sends him a message, and he writes back quickly. All afternoon, they chat back and forth about books and dating and his work as a teacher. When he asks, she tells him she works in energy and likes her job, and then she redirects him back to talking about his students. He types: *Wait, you work in energy? Like healing crystals, that kind of thing?*

Claudia laughs but does not write LOL.

Energy, like wind turbines and that kind of thing, she types back.

Thank God. I thought you were going to ask me about my sign next.

Claudia deletes what she has been typing.

They chat online until it is very late and Claudia feels her eyes drooping.

I wish I didn't have to work in the morning, she writes, and means it. Daniel asks for her phone number. He says he will call her the next night around seven, after they're both home from work, and he types [*goodnight kiss*]. She blows a kiss at the screen, feeling hope rumbling around inside her like hunger. It propels her through Monday with some of her old energy. She gets up without hitting snooze and turns the water to cold. She does up her blouse, brushes on mascara, and pulls on her tall boots without dread for the day.

At the office, she puts together a PowerPoint on industry best practices. She meets with one of the project managers to review welding procedures. She drinks her usual one cup of Earl Grey in the afternoon and only yawns a few times. By five, the rumble has become a hum.

Before leaving the plant, she checks her personal email. There's an email from her sister and a forwarded video from June. And something from Leon. Curious, she clicks to open it. There's no text and most of the image is grey: a mushroom cloud blooming over a desecrated landscape, pocked by naked trees and collapsed buildings. The only bits of colour are shards of what appears to be a cut-up photo. The bits are coming out of the cloud. Something about the colours is familiar. Claudia leans closer and recognizes a necklace in one shard and part of her own eye in another. Leon has sliced her profile photo up into nuclear rain.

She forwards Leon's email to June, and as she packs up to leave, she thinks this will be a funny story to tell Daniel when he calls. But settling underneath the layer of her that finds this funny is a sediment of alarm.

By midnight, Claudia is angry at herself for being hopeful when experience has taught her the wisdom of caution. She checks her email before she goes to bed, but there is nothing from Daniel. Nothing from Leon either. Only a one-line note from June: *Enough now. If you don't call the internet people, I will.* Claudia shuts the laptop and gets into bed, so tired her eyelids hurt from staying open, but it is hours before she is able to sleep.

Claudia is sitting on a bench near the lake with her tea. Seagulls nag each other in sharp screeches.

"I hate that guy too," June says on the phone.

"It's fine," Claudia sighs. "I don't really want to talk about it."

Actually, it's not that Claudia doesn't want to talk about it so much as she doesn't want to hear about it. She doesn't want to hear all the possibilities about where Daniel has disappeared to—he's on a week-long field trip with his class, his dog is near death and he's been with him in the vet hospital, he deleted the part of the chat with her phone number in it by accident. These options are not plausible and not comforting, even though June means well.

"Well, it's not fine as far as I'm concerned, but you've got bigger problems. Did you contact the website about Leon yet?"

"I will do it, I promise."

"There's something wrong with that guy, and it's your responsibility to make sure he doesn't have a chance to blow up on somebody else."

Claudia yawns.

"I need to get back to work. I'll let them know about Leon. I'll talk to you later, okay?"

She ends the call and takes a sip from her Styrofoam cup. The last of her tea is cold. She pulls off the lid and tosses what's left of it at the seagulls, but it doesn't even get close, and some of the cold tea splashes on her leg, and she feels like crying but nothing happens.

Claudia's assistant is standing in the doorway.

"You've got that meeting with Rick and Carlos in five minutes."

"Oh!"

"You forgot?"

"No," Claudia says, but it's obvious that she has.

"Want me to postpone?

"Uh ..." Claudia can't remember who booked this meeting or why.

"I think I'd better." Laura's expression is probably smug, but it might be concerned, or both. Claudia doesn't look at her long enough to figure it out.

"Sure, thanks," Claudia says and shuts the door behind her so she can read her email in peace.

There is something from Leon. The text of the message has been cut out of magazines like he's asking for a ransom in the eighties, which would be funny if the message said something different.

People like you are why the world is ending.

What scares Claudia the most is the feeling that Leon somehow knows her. It feels like he can see right inside her to all the grey, murky parts she keeps out of sight, all the icky, evil, squirmy things that she thinks about other people and herself. He is the only one who sees how she really is, and he hates her.

Claudia leaves a message for her boss saying she's sick. She emails Laura to tell her she won't be in today, and puts the phone under the pillow she isn't using. She turns over and goes back to sleep.

She dreams she is drinking a pint of beer, but no matter how many sips she takes the glass doesn't get any emptier. She is sitting on a park bench in a bar she hasn't been in before, and the waiter keeps coming over to check on her progress.

"You can't leave until you finish that," he says. The waiter has

Daniel's profile picture eyes and Leon's tight, angry mouth. "I'm trying," Claudia tries to tell him, but the words are lodged in her mouth until he's already walked away. She looks around for June—she has a vague feeling that she was supposed to meet June here, at this strange bar she doesn't remember arriving at. But there's just the waiter and a few other empty park benches. Is she at the wrong place? She takes three gulps of beer—warm and flat—and holds up her glass to check on her progress, whether she's any closer to being able to leave. The amber liquid sloshes over the lip of the glass onto her hand and hisses. There is something floating in there. She holds the beer up higher so it's infused with the light behind it, and it's full of ripped-up pieces of paper, and she looks over to tell the waiter, but he's gone and the bar is grey and disintegrating, the stools shrivelling down to ash, and Claudia is so terrified she wakes up.

CALL ME NOW says the subject heading of an email from Laura. The message is blank. Claudia is exhausted but afraid to go back to sleep, the aftertaste of the dream in her throat. She was checking her email from her laptop to make sure there's nothing at work she needs to attend to and apparently there is. She pulls the phone from under the pillow and walks into the kitchen. She puts the kettle on and looks at her phone. Five missed calls: three from Laura, one from her boss at the plant, and a number she doesn't recognize.

"Finally!" Laura says instead of *hello*.

"What is it?"

"You are so lucky you're sick today. It's chaos here!" It sounds like Laura is outside. Claudia can hear seagulls and voices.

"Where are you?"

"We're all down the street from the plant. Somebody called in a bomb threat!"

Claudia's stomach clenches. Her mouth is filling with spit.

"What?"

"I know, right? It's crazy." Laura sounds excited.

If there is a bomb in the plant, Laura isn't safe down the street.

Claudia isn't safe in her apartment. Evacuating is like spitting on a forest fire. Laura, like a kid under a desk, is probably getting a kick out of this unprecedented disruption in routine. Claudia sees her, phone to her ear, falling to ash. Seagulls dropping into dust. Claudia's bed and kettle and computer, all crumbling apart in an instant. Claudia herself, disintegrating.

"Is it a bomb?" she chokes out.

"Nah, they don't think so. They're checking again, but they think it's just a threat."

Claudia breathes and prays a thank you, but she is still afraid.

"You there?"

"Yes. Who called it in?"

"They don't know," Laura says, but Claudia can hear June's voice telling her to call the internet people, and a film of guilt settles over her, grey and fine as nuclear ash. The kettle starts to scream.

On Walnut Street

ALICE SAW THE FOR-SALE SIGN AT LUCIA'S AS SOON AS SHE walked into the front room to drink her tea in peace. It was only a week after the dinner party. Across the street, the driveway was empty and the curtains were drawn. Alice dressed and let herself out of the house quietly while the children and Howard were banging around at breakfast. She went over and knocked on Lucia's door. The potted crocus was gone from the windowsill.

Everybody was talking about it at the Andersens' get-together the next Saturday.

"Can you believe it? Right in the middle of the school year, too!" Mary swirled her drink, and the ice cubes clinked together.

"I knew something was weird about them, right from the beginning," Lorna said. "They never fit in here."

Maureen bit into a hot dog. Ketchup dripped out of the end of the bun and splotched onto the linoleum between her espadrilles.

"Maybe they moved for the Eyetalian's work or something," she said, her mouth full.

Lorna flinched. "Sure. Maybe. But that's not what I heard."

"What did you hear?" Mary looked up from her drink and stared at Lorna.

"Think about it, Mary. They're Italian, right? They move here suddenly and move away a few months later, with no warning at all? Didn't you see *The Godfather*?"

Mary shrugged.

Maureen swallowed the bite of hot dog. Her eyes were big. "You mean you think they're in the mafia?"

"Congratulations on catching up, Maureen. I'm not saying they're part of it, not necessarily, but I think they're mixed up in all that bad business somehow."

"Maybe they're on the run," Mary said, but she sounded skeptical.

"Maybe." Lorna looked pleased with herself as she brushed crumbs off the front of her sleeveless blouse.

"Can I get anyone something to drink?" Alice asked. "I'm going to see if they can make a martini."

The other women shook their heads. Lorna stared at her.

"You're very fancy all of a sudden, Alice Cartwright," she said, smiling like it could have been a joke.

When Lucia waved to Alice from her front yard, she always called out, "Hello, Mrs." Not *Alice* or *Mrs. Cartwright*. Just *Mrs.* In the six months they lived across from each other on Walnut Street, Lucia called Alice by her first name only once.

"Hello there, Loo-chee-ah," Alice would say, pronouncing each syllable. Lucia was beautiful. When she bent down to pick up the paper from the front porch, she did it in one gentle swoop, as if she were a fish moving through water. Her skin was smooth, too; she might be twenty-five, but Alice imagined her to be closer to forty. Lucia's eyes were brown, like Alice's, but there was something bigger and more dramatic about Lucia's. When she blinked or closed her eyes in thought, her lashes folded down over them, as smooth as her newspaper swoop. Her long, blond hair was usually held half up in a clip, off her face but still streaming down her back. She must be very rare in Italy, Alice thought the first time they met and she heard the woman's accent as she introduced herself. The other neighbours on the street called her the Eyetalian's Blond Wife.

Lucia had two tall, quiet children, a boy and a girl. Both had blond hair cropped short. The girl's was a pixie cut, like Mia Farrow's. It was sharp and stylish on Lucia's daughter, but Alice was secretly glad that her own girls seemed to be keeping their hair long, for now.

Lucia's girl blushed and ducked her head when Alice saw her on the street. Her skin was pale and reddened quickly, and it was probably for the best that she didn't seem to sunbathe. Not like Sheila and Cynthia, who were always lying out back in the summer, hair piled up on top of their heads, browning their lithe bodies in the sun until their father hollered at them to come in and help their mother already. Then one of them would yell back, "Dad, we're on vacation!" And this back and forth would go on for a few minutes until the girls dragged themselves inside, stomping their bare feet, leaving bits of grass on the linoleum.

Lucia's boy was younger, maybe twelve when the family moved in. He was about the same height as Peter and Danny, even though they were teenagers. He nodded at Alice when he saw her and waved at the kids but kept to himself. When Lucia's family first moved onto Walnut Street, Alice asked her children to invite the kids along to things, and Danny tried. Alice once watched Danny call after the boy as he walked towards the corner. It was early fall and the air was turning, so Alice was seeing this through a closed window and couldn't hear what the boys were saying. After a minute or two, Danny turned back to where his brother and the other neighbourhood boys were waiting. Lucia's boy walked away.

She wasn't convinced her daughters had made much of an effort at all with Lucia's girl. "We asked her over, Ma. She turned red and said no. What are we supposed to do? Drag her over here by her short hair?" Cynthia said. Sheila snorted. Alice turned away in case she couldn't adjust her face in time, in case her daughters caught her glint of dislike for them.

That Christmas, the doorbell rang when Alice was basting the turkey. Howard was asleep on the chesterfield, and the boys were playing hockey on the Andersens' backyard rink. Upstairs, Cynthia said something, and Sheila clomped across the floor.

"Girls!" Alice called as she slid the turkey back into the oven. "Can one of you get the door?"

"We're in the middle of something, Mom!" Sheila yelled.

Alice sighed. It was easier to answer the door herself. At least the girls weren't wandering into the kitchen, scavenging snacks and spoiling their dinner.

She wiped her hands on her apron and walked to the front door, the shag carpet soft on her bare feet.

"Happy Christmas, Mrs." Lucia's blond hair was stuffed under a white hat that could have been cashmere. Alice pushed her bangs out of her eyes, her hair wet from sweat and stinking of turkey heat. The winter air made her shiver. She looked down. Lucia was holding a bottle of wine, the green glass of the bottle dark against her white gloves.

"Thank you, Lucia. Merry Christmas to you too." Alice smiled, waiting.

"This is for you and your family." Lucia held out the bottle.

"That's so sweet of you. Thank you," Alice said, wiping her hands again before taking the wine. For a second, as it changed hands, the bottle slipped. Alice's heart sped up like it used to when the children were younger and she was always averting near accidents: milk on the grey chesterfield and ketchup on Sunday dresses. But Lucia didn't let go until she had a good grip. Alice's heartbeat slowed.

"Do you want to come in?" Alice asked after a pause.

"No, no thank you. I must go back." Lucia turned away.

Alice thanked her again and watched Lucia glide across the street and delicately sidestep a snow bank, tall boots black as piano legs.

Over dinner, Howard examined the label. He raised his eyebrows at Alice.

"This is really expensive stuff. Better than the fruitcake we got from the Andersens for sure."

Alice nodded as she swallowed a mouthful of turnip mash. Howard put the unopened bottle back on the table and got himself a beer from the fridge.

At the Carlisles' New Year's party, Alice stood in the kitchen with the other neighbourhood women.

"We invited the Eyetalians," Mary Carlisle said as she finished mixing herself an old fashioned at the makeshift bar beside the sink.

"And?" asked Lorna.

"She said thanks, but no thanks, of course," Mary said, stirring her drink with the handle of a spoon.

"Of course," said Maureen.

"Big surprise. Has anybody even seen the Eyetalian? I bet it's just her over there with the kids." Lorna shook her glass and tipped it up, sliding an ice cube into her mouth.

"Nobody's seen him?" Alice asked, stepping out of the way as Lorna reached past her to pull a bottle of vodka from the freezer.

"She has." Maureen pointed at Mary with her elbow.

"I told you that, Lorna," Mary said, watching Lorna refill her glass.

"So you saw him ..." Alice prompted.

"Very early in the morning, driving away in that flashy Cadillac. Not much to look at, but he definitely exists," said Mary.

"Do you know we brought casseroles over to the Eyetalian's Blond Wife that first week they moved in? Not even a thank-you note. Let alone returning the favour when Artie's mother died." Lorna pinched her lips together over her straw and slurped.

"Maybe they're shy," Alice said.

"Maybe. But a gesture of neighbourly goodwill every once in a while wouldn't kill her," Lorna said.

"They brought us wine on Christmas," Alice said, quietly.

"What?" said Maureen just as Mary was saying, "Pardon me?"

"Lucia brought us wine on Christmas," Alice repeated.

"You're kidding. Did you get any wine, Lorna?" Mary said.

"Of course not."

"Me neither," chimed in Maureen.

The three women looked at Alice. She wished she hadn't mentioned it.

"I mean, it's probably just because the kids are close in age." Alice poked at a lime slice in her glass with a swizzle stick.

"Did you give them a bottle of wine when they moved in?" Lorna asked.

The women waited.

"We did, yes," Alice lied.

"Well," Lorna said. "That must be it then."

In the other room, the men were laughing. Alice listened to see if she could pick out Howard's voice, but the sounds of the husbands blended together, indistinct.

It was later in January when Alice first saw Lucia's husband. January was miserable that year, blustery and relentless. Snow piled up in the driveways overnight, the winter laying down its white blankets again as soon as the men removed them.

On the morning after the first big snowfall, Alice was in the kitchen early, making tea for herself before the kids got up and came downstairs wanting breakfast. Howard was pushing the snow to the edge of the driveway and heaving it into the yard.

Across the street, Lucia's husband walked slowly down the steps of his house, one gloved hand holding a shovel, the other one gripping onto the snow-covered banister. He was shorter than Howard and twice as wide, even with Howard's post-Christmas bulge filling out his blue parka. Like a snowman, his pale, round face melted into his middle sphere, uninterrupted by neck. His head was bare despite the cold, and his thick hair was as black as barbeque charcoals.

Howard called out something. From the bottom of the steps, Lucia's husband waved and smiled, saying something back that Alice couldn't hear. Then he bent and started clearing the path in the direction of the sidewalk, small shovelfuls half the size of Howard's. He was still shovelling when Howard came inside, stamping the snow off his boots.

"Howard?" Alice called softly, not wanting the children to wake up yet. She went to the front door, pulling her bathrobe around her more tightly.

"Morning, Alice," Howard said, bending down to untie his boots.

"Honey, before you take your boots off, can you go back out

there and help him?" The front door was open, and through the screen door Alice could see Lucia's husband labouring, his round face red.

Howard sighed. "He does look like he's having a rough time of it, doesn't he? Poor bastard."

He tightened his laces and pulled his hat down over his ears.

"You're a sweet man." Alice put her hands on Howard's shoulders and leaned in to kiss his cheek, his skin cold and smelling of outside.

Howard pulled the door shut behind him. Alice watched them from the kitchen, sipping her tea. Her husband slowed down his shovelling speed, letting the other man lead.

By the time Howard sat down at the table, his face was red too. The children were awake, stomping around upstairs and jostling each other for time in the bathroom. Alice put an extra slice of bacon on Howard's plate and kissed him on his bald spot.

The next day, a teenager Alice didn't recognize came to shovel Lucia's driveway and did so for the rest of the winter, thin and fast, more efficient than Howard even. Some mornings Sheila and Cynthia got up early to watch the boy, giggling in the kitchen. On those mornings, Alice finished her tea in the living room.

Spring came slowly. It was mid-April when the crocuses beside the driveway pushed themselves up out of the dirty snow. One Monday, Alice was crouching next to them and peering at the flowers when she heard, "Mrs.!"

Alice stood up too quickly and her head felt fuzzy and strange. She rubbed her face.

"You okay, Mrs.?" Lucia's brown eyes squinted, from concern or the sun.

"I'm fine. Thanks, Lucia."

"Angelo and I, we would like to invite you and your husband to have dinner at our home, this Saturday evening?" With Lucia's head tilted, her blond hair was longer on one side, brushing her inner left elbow.

Lorna would be furious. Alice smiled.

"We'd love to. What can we bring?"

"Do not bring anything. I will have the dinner prepared." Lucia bent down close to the crocuses. "These are very beautiful."

Lucia brushed the snow away from the base of the plants, making her hands wet and more green visible. Alice knew what she would bring Lucia on Saturday.

"Will Saturday be an adults-only evening?"

Lucia wrinkled her nose and frowned as if she were trying to sort out Alice's words.

"What I mean is, should we bring the children or no?"

"If you want it, of course, but my children are going to the cinema that night."

Perfect. "Perfect," Alice said. "It will be just Howard and me, then."

Alice's hands were getting cold, wrapped around the green pot in its crinkly silver wrapping. Howard rang the bell again.

"Why didn't you just give her one from the yard?" Howard asked.

"It's nicer this way. Actually, I don't even know if a wild crocus can survive once you've dug it up and transplanted it."

The door opened and Lucia stood in a billowy gold top draped over tailored white slacks, radiant.

"Are we early?" asked Alice.

"You are here at a good time. Come in!" Lucia opened the door wide.

Alice wiped her feet on the mat at the door. Everything in the hallway was white: gleaming tile under their feet and bright walls that smelled like they'd just been painted. Alice marvelled at how neat the entranceway was: no kicked-off shoes or dropped handbags. No children's coats. She made a mental note to tidy the front hall when she got home.

Howard leaned against the wall to take his shoes off.

"No, no. Please. Leave them," Lucia said.

They followed her down the hall. Still holding the crocus, Alice glanced at the wall to see if Howard had left a handprint, but there was nothing there.

In the living room, Howard made a beeline for a black leather easy chair. Alice stepped toward Lucia to give her the potted plant.

"Oh! So beautiful!" Lucia said, her eyebrow arcs lifting in delight. She took the purple crocus and put it on the windowsill facing the street.

Lucia's husband, Angelo, came into the room then, dressed in black pants that were a little too short. Alice could see two thick strips of white sock above his black shoes, like the cream between Oreos. His black shirt was unbuttoned at the neck, showing a patch of curly, silver hairs. Alice looked away.

"Howard!" A smile split Angelo's wide, red face in half as Howard stood up and the two men shook hands.

"Mrs." Angelo took Alice's hand and kissed it. She blushed and perched at the end of the black leather chesterfield. Angelo sat at the other end, leaning forward to talk to Howard. Lucia disappeared. When she came back, she was holding a silver platter of drinks. There were six glasses.

"Is someone else joining us? Another couple?" Alice turned back toward the front door to cover her disappointment.

Lucia shook her head and her hair caught the light.

"Oh no, Mrs.," she said. "I have some extra drinks here. I didn't know what you wanted, you and Mr." Lucia pointed her chin towards Howard, who selected a beer from the tray, as usual. Angelo took a beer for himself. After studying what was left—two highball glasses of something reddish, a tumbler of what could have been scotch, and a martini glass with clear liquid and three olives—Alice chose the martini, which she'd never had before but had seen in the movies. Lucia put the tray down on the small side table before taking the scotch for herself and sitting down beside Alice.

"We will eat dinner after our drinks."

Alice tried to sniff the air discreetly to see what Lucia was cooking, but she couldn't smell anything at all.

"It is so nice for you to come here and eat with us. You are the first friends we have to dinner," said Angelo.

"Really?" Howard raised his eyebrows.

Angelo cleared his throat and looked embarrassed. "My wife, she is very wonderful, but she is not a cook." Angelo smiled at his wife. Alice wondered if Lucia would get angry, but she only laughed and leaned down to kiss Angelo on the top of his head.

The husbands talked about the weather and basketball. Howard didn't really follow basketball, but he seemed to be keeping up his end of the conversation. Howard always seemed relaxed in social situations, even when he wasn't. Sometimes Alice watched him from the edges of parties and admired his stretched-out legs, his easy grin, and envied him.

"How are your children?" Lucia asked.

"Oh, they're all fine, really," Alice said. "And yours?"

"They are fine, also."

The women sat together quietly. Lucia looked over at the crocus, its green leaves pressed up against the glass. Alice sipped her drink and squinted against the heat sliding down her throat and into her belly. She fiddled with the toothpick holding its trio of olives.

"Do you need help in the kitchen?" she asked.

"No, no. It is done." Lucia stood up.

"Come into the dining room, everybody," she said, leading the way into the room next door.

The round table was laid for four, with glinting silverware as shiny as the front hall and delicate, gold-rimmed china perfectly centred at each place. And finally, Alice could smell dinner: grease, green onions, slick chop suey. In the middle of the table was an assortment of open boxes of Chinese food. Shiny spareribs in one carton and beige fried rice speckled with bits of egg and vegetables in another. Alice sat down within arm's reach of a box of chicken balls.

As soon as everyone was seated, Lucia and her husband began digging in. Exchanging a glance, Howard and Alice did the same. Alice spooned a small helping of rice onto her gold-rimmed plate and stabbed a chicken ball with her fork, lifting it out of the box with ease but struggling to drop it onto her plate. Finally, she poked the chicken ball with her finger to dislodge it from the fork. It was ice cold. Howard was already eating and had a strange expression on his face, like when the kids used to make him their peanut-butter French toast on Father's Day. She reached for the bright sweet-and-sour sauce and poured a dollop onto the edge of her plate. It glowed there like alien blood.

The inside of the chicken ball was even colder than its puffy fried coating. Alice choked and dipped it back into the sauce to make it go down easier, but the goop was freezing and slimy and only made the whole thing taste worse. She tried some rice, and it too tasted as though it had been waiting on the table for hours. She snuck a glance at Lucia and Angelo, who were passing the cartons between them and cheerfully eating mouthfuls as they did. She checked Howard's face to see if she was just being picky, if perhaps the food was plenty hot and delicious too. Howard's face was pinched as he ploughed through his plate, head down. Alice remembered the time they went to the county fair and stopped to watch the contestants in a hot-dog eating competition, pushing the food into their mouths, gulping water to keep from vomiting. Perhaps she was not being picky. Alice managed to choke down the rest of the dry chicken ball and then spent the rest of the meal pushing the rice around her plate between gulps of martini. The martini was getting easier to drink. She wished there was another one.

They ate quietly, for a while.

"Did you see there's a new supermarket opening on Fourth?" Howard asked the table.

Lucia nodded. "Yes, it's so close to us; it's much better."

"Who is your mechanic?" Angelo asked Howard, and the discussion of mechanics took the rest of the meal: who charged what, how to get a good deal on a tune-up, whether regular oil changes could be pushed back, where the best coffee was. The husbands' talk floated over the table, out of reach.

"Mrs. Come upstairs with me? To see something," Lucia said.

Alice followed Lucia out of the room and up the carpeted steps, white too and clean as unused napkins. Lucia went into a room without furniture and glided over to the closet. She opened it and stood back so Alice could see.

The closet was half the size of the dining room, with shelves lining half of it and the rest devoted to hangers of clothes, many of them covered in dry-cleaner plastic. Lucia pointed to the neat stacks of colour. Leaning closer, Alice saw that they were piles of leather pants: red, sky blue, a startling yellow, bright orange. She had never seen so many pairs of pants in a place that wasn't a store.

"Oh my." Alice did not know what else to say.

The floor of the closet was covered with pairs of leather boots in red, black, beige, even a green pair. Lucia beamed. She reached in and pulled out a dress sheathed in plastic, which she ripped off and threw back into the closet. She held the dress against her and swayed in front of Alice.

It was gorgeous, the purple of the crocus downstairs and shot through with silvery thread. As Lucia moved, Alice saw the silver lining of the dress. The hemline stopped well above the knee. It looked like silk. Alice peered closer and saw a price tag dangling out of a sleeve: $798.

"Please take this." Lucia's eyes were darker than usual. She held the dress against Alice. "It is beautiful, no?"

"It is, Lucia, but I can't accept it." Alice tried to keep the wistfulness out of her voice.

"I know the dinner was not so good. I am a bad cook, and Angelo went to the restaurant to get us the food. It is probably not what people serve here for dinner parties."

Alice smiled. "People don't usually serve dresses instead of dessert, either."

"Please, Alice," Lucia said.

In the Andersens' kitchen, Maureen pushed the last bit of her hot dog into her mouth. Still chewing, she rubbed at a mustard stain on the sleeve of her blouse.

"You're making that worse, Maureen." Lorna rolled her eyes, but Maureen was too busy dabbing at the spreading yellow smear to notice.

Alice swirled her martini and sipped. The gin made her throat warm.

"Can you believe it?" Lorna said. "Just up and left. At least you got that bottle of wine, Alice."

"Just as well they left. Like you said, Lorna, it's not like they fit in here." Mary tipped her glass into her mouth and drained it.

Alice smoothed the skirt of her purple dress and looked out the window into the Andersens' backyard. Way at the back of the flat, brown yard, she could see a few bright green crocus heads, poking up toward the light, hopeful and out of place.

ACKNOWLEDGEMENTS

Without Helen Humphreys, this book would be a pamphlet, and nobody would be reading it except me. I'll never be able to thank her enough for reading, editing, and believing in this book. I am indebted also to Gary Draper, the only person to point out that, in fact, books don't sink. And to my sister, Sarah Higgins, who always cares about the characters and doesn't mind when I quote myself.

Thank you to everybody at Tightrope Books, especially Jim Nason and Heather Wood. Thank you both for your encouragement and for your limitless patience with my pestering ways. Thank you Deanna Janovski for your sharp eye, precision, and flexibility, and David Jang for your beautiful cover.

Thank you so much to Jessica Westhead and Catherine Bush for reading and endorsing this book. Thank you to Hayley Andoff for being a photography genius, and to Christine Cho for her makeup magic.

Thank you to my friends. Thank you for all of your support in its various forms. Thanks especially to my long-haul loves: Agnes Kowalski, Annie Muldoon, Catherine Koehler, Chris Berwick, Elisabeth Leggett Richards, Erin McElhone, Manuela Popovici and Zuzana Eperjesi. Thank you also to: Kate Henderson, Kelly Noussis, Lori Naylor, Diana Ballon, Rebekah Grayston, Deborah Deacon, Tanya McMillan, Hanne Wenkeler, Rosa Gomez, Caryn Thompson, Mark Fernley, Pauline Ho, Mary Thompson, Krista Richey, Irma Molina, Jenna Tenn-Yuk, and everybody else who has helped me in a million ways both concrete and abstract.

Thank you to my family: Andrew Higgins, Alexa Higgins, Kathy and Paul Higgins, the Wills Voogd Contingent (Julie, Gordon, Mattias, and Markus), Harvey Voogd and the rest of the Voogd family. This book is dedicated to my parents, Krystyna and Michael, and to their parents: Margaret, Joseph, Frances, and Boleslaw.

I'm grateful to the Humber School for Writers' Correspondence Program, which gave me the opportunity to work one-on-one with an established writer (spoiler alert: it was Helen) and focus on the project that became this book.

Thank you to Alison Gadsby and Junction Writes (the 2013-2014 crew: Kelly, Kate, Dolly, Chrissi, Jo, Jim, Josh, and Jam). This group of wonderful writers offered careful reading, insightful edits, and ongoing inspiration for early versions of "Windpipe," "My Dad and Me, and Everybody Else," "Charlene at Lunchtime," "What Vern Did," "Clara and Rosemary," and "On Walnut Street."

Three of these stories were published previously, in slightly different form. Thank you to the folks at the *Antigonish Review* for publishing "The Colours of Birds." Thank you also to Mike Landry at the *Saint-John Telegraph-Journal* for publishing "Everything Inside," and to the *Toronto Star* for publishing "The White Stain."

There are many people and things that inspired these stories. The movie *Pollock* (2000) first introduced me to Lee Krasner, and an exhibit at the Nova Scotia Art Gallery sparked my fascination with Maud Lewis. Thanks to all the folks I met in New Orleans. Thanks also to Mary Ching for telling me the story that turned into "On Walnut Street," and to Lori Naylor for telling me the story that became "The End of Everything Fun." Thank you to Markus for being in my family, and to Mickey for the Original Joey stories. I'm also grateful for *The Golden Girls*, Shel Silverstein's *The Giving Tree*, the TTC for its myriad of eavesdropping opportunities, and all the weirdos not otherwise mentioned.

Finally, thank you to Bruce Voogd, for co-creating Vern, for reading stories, for being wise and kind, and for making me laugh every day.

ABOUT THE AUTHOR

Rebecca Higgins has lived and worked in Ireland, Honduras, and Brazil. She has a background in social work and has worked in mental health education since 2011. Her short stories have appeared in such publications as the *Toronto Star* and the *Antigonish Review*. She lives in Toronto.